IN PLAIN SIGHT

IN PLAIN SIGHT
By Valerie Davisson
Copyright © 2022 Valerie Davisson

IN PLAIN SIGHT is a work of fiction. Names, characters, places, and incidents are the product of the author's imagination or are used fictitiously. Any resemblance to actual events, locales, businesses, or persons, living or dead, is coincidental.

Published by Vaughn House Publishing, Depoe Bay, OR
First Edition

Print ISBN - 978-1-7340119-9-9
Ebook ISBN - 979-8-9864774-0-4

Cover and Interior Design by Kimberly Peticolas, www.kimpeticolas.com

Library of Congress Control Number: 2022915295

10   9   8   7   6   5   4   3   2   1

IN PLAIN SIGHT

A Logan McKenna Novel

VALERIE DAVISSON

PROLOGUE

DECEMBER, 2021

TWO DAYS BEFORE CHRISTMAS

OLD TOWN, PORTLAND, OR

Fifteen more minutes, but that was as long as he was waiting for this asshole. The man stamped his feet on the brick pavers and shoved his hands in his armpits.

Night had fallen hours ago, but with ambient light from the traffic signal and a few neon bar signs, he could still see well enough. There wasn't much to look at. Behind him rose the empty hulk of the old Greyhound Bus Depot. He didn't know it, but in its time, it was hailed as a shining example of modern architecture, a real jewel in the city's crown. Now, stripped of its former glory, all that remained were streaked slabs of dismal gray concrete stretched across a series of darkened doorways.

It was so cold, not even the crazies were out. Not even his favorite: the old lady who ran around half naked, babbling

1

to herself, shitting in doorways, stepping on stray needles the addicts had thrown away, and not feeling a thing. Even she must have found a shelter or a tarp to curl up under on this cold night.

Come O-N . . . ! Where are you?

Five more minutes. Then, that was it. He'd leave and consider this deal dead.

Squinting past the line of tents and tarps strung along the sidewalk like grimy pearls, he considered walking around the block to keep his feet from freezing, but he didn't want to miss his customer. Besides, he didn't really need to stay on the move. He could stand right here with a sign that said, "Get your drugs here!" and not have to worry about the police. The cops never came down here unless they were called and even then, it would be a long wait. People who lived here learned to handle things themselves.

Frustrated, he stamped his feet again and blew on his fingers to keep warm. His breath came out in white puffs, swirled, then floated away in the frigid air. He remembered something from sixth grade science about condensation happening when the warm air from his mouth hit the cold air outside. He shoved his hands into his pockets and felt around. Good. The package was still there.

This better be the right stuff. His client had been very specific. The roofies were easy. He could get those any day of the week. But the other product was harder to find. Since this drug wasn't used to get high, it wasn't as readily available. Dealers tended to keep a larger supply of their customers' most desired substances on hand—heroin, meth, coke, Oxy, and E, whatever made them feel good or at least made the real world fade away . . . for a little while.

Yes, the order had been hard to fill, but he took pride in being able to procure anything his customers desired. He had connections. And this customer was a regular. Paid in cash. Never a problem.

Finally, there was movement at the end of the street. He watched as his customer, dressed in dark pants, boots, and a hoodie, deftly stepped around a blue tent at the end of the row and continued at a deliberate pace toward him.

By all means, take your sweet time . . . I've only been out here freezing my ass off for the last hour, waiting for you . . .

He knew better than to voice his complaints out loud. This was business and even though business was good, he couldn't afford to lose any.

Let's just get this done.

Without bothering with the niceties (or an apology for being late), product and cash were exchanged efficiently. No need to ask after each other's families or how the Trailblazers were doing this year. They were there for one reason and one reason only. Even though cops rarely patrolled this area, there was no sense hanging around. He had survived this long by not taking unnecessary risks.

He watched until his customer turned the corner. He wondered again about the unusual request. Out of curiosity, he had researched the product when he got the order—it was very specific. Had to be the injectable form. It was used in a variety of ways, some to relieve suffering, some to cause it. To hurt or to heal? He wondered which of those end results his customer had in mind. Gave him the creeps. Maybe he should stop doing business with this one after all.

Shoving the cash deeper into his pocket, the dealer pulled his wool beanie down tighter over his ears and crossed the street, heading for his own neighborhood. He had money in his pocket and the night was young. He'd long ago learned not to indulge in his own product. Tequila was his drug of choice, and he had the rest of the night to enjoy it.

1

"Woohoo!"

Logan looked out the kitchen window and saw Sam dancing up the driveway, holding aloft two wiggly-clawed Dungeness crabs, one in each hand, all while valiantly trying to keep her hot-pink, rhinestone encrusted, cat-eye glasses from sliding off her nose. The crabs were very much alive, but the tiny woman kept a firm hold, gripping them expertly from the bottom so their sharp claws couldn't reach her fingers or any other part of her anatomy.

Sam was Samantha B. Pullman, reporter for the local weekly paper, the News Times. She and her husband, Tim, owned a small crab boat, which had just returned from its first trip of the season. For the first time in forever, the boats were going out on time and for one of the best prices for crab they'd ever negotiated.

After offloading their catch, Tim and his crew went right back out, but he'd sent some celebratory crustaceans over with

Sam for what he'd dubbed *the Cormorant Coffee Crew* to enjoy. The CCC consisted of Sam, Logan, and Jean, Tim's sister. Tim was an honorary member.

Before moving to Oregon, Logan had never heard of cormorants, but learned the ubiquitous long-necked seabirds, found all along the Oregon coast, were so successful at diving and catching their dinner that they were considered good luck charms by the fishermen. Last Christmas, Sam gave them each a mug with a cormorant on one side and their name on the other. They used them every time they got together.

Tim's sister, Jean Pullman was not only the Lincoln County Medical Examiner, but had a full-time practice in Lincoln City, just north of Depoe Bay. The three women became friends a year ago while working to keep a young man out of jail for a murder he didn't commit. Sam and Logan met for breakfast burritos at Pirate's Coffee every Wednesday and Jean joined them whenever her patients—dead or alive—didn't require her immediate attention.

Sam danced back to the truck and returned the two crabs to the cooler to party with their friends until bath time. She deftly kicked the tailgate shut before struggling up the walk with the cooler, her glasses securely back in place . . . for now.

"Wow! Those are huge!" Logan called out the window before drying her hands and going to help her in the front door. "How many are in there?"

She almost felt guilty that her own contribution to the meal consisted of a bowl of coleslaw, but even that had stretched her limited culinary skills. Except for the roast chicken her French foreign-exchange mother had insisted she learn to make, Logan was more of an assembler than a cook.

Jean was bringing the bread—fresh sourdough from Depoe Baykery over in Salishan. Only the best, of course. Jean did pretty much everything to perfection.

IN PLAIN SIGHT

Sam hauled the cooler onto the counter next to the sink and went back to get the crab pot from the truck. Logan didn't own a pot large enough. When she saw her carrying it back, Logan was grateful her gas range was built into the island and not in the counter under the cupboards. Otherwise, it would never have fit.

"I never got you a housewarming present," Sam said over her shoulder as she filled the pot with water in the sink. "Besides, no self-respecting friend of a fisherman doesn't have a crab pot—now you no longer have to live in shame," she grinned, tucking a curve of shiny, jet-black hair behind her ear.

"Thank you," Logan said, wondering where she was going to store it when they were done. Probably out in the garage. Still, it was nice to be welcomed into the fold. Her husband, Ben, would know what to do with it. He was the cook in the family.

Sam lit the burner under the pot. They had plenty of time to visit before that amount of water came to a boil.

"Now, point me to the beer!"

Logan handed her a Rogue Brewery Knuckle Buster IPA from the fridge on the way and grabbed one for herself. Jean always stuck to wine.

"Did I get the right one?" Logan asked as Sam looked at the label.

In answer, Sam smiled, popped the tab, took a long drink, sitting down in one of the two big chairs in the living room bookending the fireplace.

"Ahhhh," she said, toasting Logan with the half emptied can.

"So how's Tim? Is he satisfied with the first run/load/catch/ trip out?" Logan said, settling into the other chair. She wasn't sure what the correct fishing lingo was.

"Oh, yeah! It was a great haul," Sam said. "The whole crew is exhausted, but it's all worth it. Everyone's bank accounts are going to look a lot healthier in a few weeks, including ours."

"*And*," she added, answering Logan's first question, "even better, no accidents reported so far. Weather's holding. Let's hope it stays that way."

Logan didn't know much about commercial fishing, but she had tried to educate herself about what her neighbors did for a living since she and Ben had bought the house in Depoe Bay and were spending more and more time up here on the Oregon coast.

Crabbing season officially opened December 1 each year, but for several years the start of the season had been delayed either to domoic acid levels being too high (Logan had no idea what domoic acid was, but she assumed high levels were bad for you) or there not being enough meat on the crabs. The fishermen had been taking a big financial hit not just from the delay of the season, but from low prices.

This year, for the first time in a long time, all the stars aligned. The weather was good, the crabs meaty, levels of domoic acid low, and the opening day price was the highest ever negotiated with the processing plant. Everyone was ecstatic when the season opened yesterday, December 1, right on schedule.

"Well then, tonight, we celebrate!" Logan said, raising her beer in a toast.

Later, when Jean arrived and Logan got up to let her in, she realized how late it had gotten. Sometime while she and Sam were catching up, the sun had gone down and a gusty rain shower was gaining momentum.

Without meaning to, Jean always made an entrance. A few inches taller than Logan, she appeared even more statuesque due to her elegant updo, accented by what she called her skunk stripe, a natural white streak that swept boldly through her thick, black hair. From the top of her French twist to the tips of her manicured nails, the woman was always impeccable.

Carrying a stylish, leather bag with two bottles of wine poking out the top and exuding the tantalizing aroma of fresh, sourdough bread, Jean wiped her feet on the mat and gave Logan a hug. Shrugging off her cashmere coat, she strode into the kitchen.

Trailing behind, Logan took note of today's shoes—low-heeled leather boots in an electric blue—very expensive looking. She'd rarely seen her repeat a footwear selection. Her shoes were the only bright spot Jean allowed in her otherwise black and white wardrobe. Somehow, her boots had made it from the car to the house in pristine condition. Nary a mud splatter or drop of water on them.

How did she do that?

"Sorry I'm late," Jean said. "Had a last-minute emergency."

2

Logan covered the kitchen table with newspaper and gave each of them a big plate, plenty of napkins, and crab crackers to get into their dinner. When the water boiled, Sam put in the seasonings and the crab. While they waited, Jean finished telling them about her last patient of the day.

"Kid bounced right off mom's lap and landed face first on the corner of the loan officer's desk at the bank. Busted his top lip. Put his front tooth right through it."

With her brusque and efficient bedside manner, Jean was revered more than loved, but was always there for her patients. There was never less than a three-month wait to get in to see Jean.

"Jeez, is he okay?" Logan asked, putting the bread on the table.

"Why didn't she catch him before he hit the desk?" Sam asked.

"Yes, he's fine, just needed a few stitches," Jean said, opening the Daisy Creek Viognier she brought and pouring herself and Logan a glass. Sam still had her beer.

"And to answer your question, Sam, the mom is eight-and-a-half-months pregnant. I doubt she could reach that far once he launched."

"Why?" asked Sam, who had no children and wasn't planning on having any. Presumably, Tim didn't want kids either. "Why would he do that?"

"Who knows why a two-year-old does anything," Jean said, taking a sip of her wine. "You really should try this, Sam."

"No, thanks. I don't drink anything I can't pronounce," Sam said, grabbing another beer.

"Did they at least get the loan?" Logan deadpanned.

"That, I don't know," Jean laughed.

An hour later, stuffed with crab and happily mellowed by their respective beverages, they cleaned up and adjourned to the living room for a slice of chocolate cake and coffee. One thing Logan always had on hand was dessert. It may be store bought, but sugar was sugar. No one complained.

Licking the thick frosting off the fork, Sam turned to Logan and asked, "So how's the old ball and chain?"

Logan laughed. She and Ben had only been married since June, but Sam had started in on the married people jokes right after they'd returned from their honeymoon. Which had been marvelous. Two weeks on the Big Island. Nothing but hiking, swimming, good food, and a good mattress. All of the honeymoon essentials.

"He's alive and well," she said, with faux politeness, "thanks for asking."

"When's he coming back? You scare him off already?" Sam asked, wiggling her eyebrows.

Before Logan could think of a good comeback, Jean said, "Well, I think you two have figured out the perfect system. Here for a while, there for a while. I'll bet more marriages would last if husbands and wives took a break from each other now and then."

IN PLAIN SIGHT

Jean's husband, Lee, was also a doctor, an orthopedist. Their jobs came with built in breaks. They did take at least one annual vacation. Ardent baseball fans, last year's trip was to spring training camp in Arizona. They seemed to be very happy.

"Well, we're still working out the details," Logan said. "Right now, Ben's down in Jasper training one of his nephews, Calvin, to take over his landscaping business. He's going to let him manage it when he's up here, and somewhere down the line, give it to him when he's ready."

"Wow, that's generous," Sam said. "Does the kid know anything about the business?"

"He'd better; he just graduated with a degree in landscape architecture from Berkeley," Logan said. "He and Trent, his brother, worked with Ben off and on during the summers when they were in high school, so he already knows a lot. They're good kids."

Jean hadn't had a chance to talk with her brother before he went back out, so she asked Sam how his first run went. While Sam was filling her in, Logan sat back and just enjoyed being there, listening. Curled up in her chair, warmed by the fire, listening to the wind and rain assail the house while they were tucked safely inside.

She was very lucky and knew it.

"So how's the video doing?" Sam asked.

The question jolted Logan out of her reverie. While her mind was wandering, the conversation had turned to the music video one of her students had pieced together from clips of her playing her violin, Bella, and put it up on YouTube. It quickly went viral and made Logan a lot of money. She'd been able to pay off her own house, as well as a large chunk of her daughter Amy's house down in Jasper. Her original starter home had already been paid off by the sale of the business after

Jack died. She'd even been able to start a college fund for her grandson, Ian.

"The first one's starting to wind down, but I'm working on some new pieces now. I'll probably schedule a recording session when I go down this spring," she said.

"Well, don't go down too soon. I was going to ask if you'd housesit for a few weeks to babysit the remodel if it needs it," Jean said. "If you're going to be in town. Probably sometime after the holidays."

Jean and her husband had several student rental properties in Eugene near the University of Oregon campus. They'd just bought another one and were in the process of making plans to fix it up.

"Sure, be happy to," Logan said. "Since I own the sound studio, I can move the schedule around as needed."

Ben and friends had converted her tiny, one-car, standalone garage into a recording studio downstairs and offices for Logan upstairs. From there she ran her music/math program called Fractals that served students in both California and Oregon.

"Tilly's running Fractals so well I hardly need to show up at all," Logan laughed.

Tilly, a trim dynamo and former high school music teacher, rented Logan's place and ran the show while she was away. When she was in town, Logan slept in a Murphy bed she'd installed in the office above the studio.

Ben's house was right behind hers, so it was convenient for everyone. She and Ben had yet to decide exactly how to merge their properties and lives together, but neither were too worried about it. They kept kicking that can down the road.

"Are the kids coming up for Christmas?" Jean asked. "They taking the shuttle?"

"Yes, and no," Logan said. "They'll be here for about a week, but they're renting a car. They had a bad experience with that shuttle and this way they have their own wheels while they're here. They're getting a full-size SUV, complete with massive car seat and movies."

It always amazed Logan how much gear and activities children required now. When she was raising Amy, all she needed was a diaper bag and a working knowledge of a number of road trip games like I Spy or the license plate hunt. A baggie of Cheerios and raisins and they were set.

"Speaking of music . . . ," Sam pointed at Bella, where she hung on the wall, glowing in the firelight. "One for the road?" Jean nodded. This had become something of a routine when they got together at her place.

Lifting Bella down and tucking her under her chin, Logan closed her eyes and slowly drew the bow across the D string, pulling them into a medley of Scottish laments she knew Sam liked. She wasn't ready to share her new stuff yet.

Outside, blocking the beams of the waning gibbous moon, a barred owl perched on the branch of a Sitka spruce, scanning the forest floor. He hooted once—in harmony or protest, it wasn't clear—swooped down and snatched a mouse in its talons, then glided silently into the trees.

3

Yes, Evka had slipped. That was bad, but Evka was a woman and women were weak. He knew she had not initiated it. Women did not have the same needs as men. Women were built different. Designed by God to be nurturers, helpmeets, and kind caregivers.

And Evka was all of that. He had watched her long, graceful fingers tenderly nurse injured raptors while softly soothing them with her velvet voice. Her thick hair, which she kept in a modest braid, was naturally dark. No dye. She didn't wear makeup, either. She didn't need to. Her skin was fair and pale. Beautiful Evka. Inside and out.

She must have been lonely when she gave in to his advances, that's all. Women were emotional creatures. She would never have gone looking for sex. That man had taken advantage of her vulnerability, her obvious sadness, that's all. And another reason this wasn't her fault. He had never told her how he felt. If he had, he was sure she wouldn't have allowed herself to become prey.

Some other man must have broken Evka's heart in Africa. He could see it in her eyes when she arrived. Like a true queen, she kept her sorrows to herself, but he knew. He could see it. He had plenty of sorrows of his own.

That's when he knew they were meant for each other. But unlike Aaron, he was a gentleman, a patient knight in shining armor. He would wait until Evka was ready.

That man hadn't. He and Evka had worked late together one night, and something must have happened, because he felt the tension between them the next morning.

He might never have known what happened, but he'd been in ward 3 and overheard her telling him in her office that "last night was a mistake that she would not let happen again."

And she hadn't. She was still his queen. He would continue to pave the way, to make himself invaluable to her, to meet her emotional needs so that then she would meet his physical ones. That's how it worked with men and women. True gentlemen needed to be patient.

*****

That had been seven months ago. He'd been patient, but tonight he would tell her how he felt. He had done the work, like Jacob laboring for seven more years for Rachel. Tonight, he would make Evka his.

As he pulled into the parking lot of the restaurant, he realized he was nervous. Well, this was an important night, he told himself. He reviewed the last year in his mind. Yes, Evka had fallen, but he was partly to blame. After all, he'd never told her how he felt. If he had, that man would not have had a chance to corrupt her. But forgive and forget. He had done the first, easily, and tonight, he would succeed with the second part of that commandment if he could. Clean slate.

IN PLAIN SIGHT

Checking his hair in the rearview mirror, he smoothed it one last time. He reached for the flowers he'd bought her, but then changed his mind and placed them back on the passenger seat. He didn't want to overwhelm her. This was supposed to be an accidental meeting, a happy coincidence. 'Oh, hello, Evka. I didn't know you liked this restaurant. I often stop here after work. Mind if I join you?'

She almost always ate out on the way home. Tuesdays was usually Gino's. Neon grape vines twined over the main entrance. He'd already checked the menu out online and selected the wine. He was leaving nothing to chance. If all went well, he would give her the flowers after dinner.

He parked far enough away that she wouldn't realize he had followed her. He waited until she got out of her car and started walking toward the restaurant before he opened his own door. He had one foot on the gravel when he noticed that instead of continuing toward the lighted entrance, Evka turned left behind the first row of cars.

With a sense of foreboding, he carefully pulled his foot back inside and the car door slowly shut until the roof light went off. Why wasn't she going inside? Was she meeting someone? That would ruin everything! He couldn't make any progress with Evka if she had a friend there, gabbing away about whatever it was women gabbed about.

In the next minute, his fears were confirmed. A large, dumpy woman got out of her car and walked back to get Evka. What happened next was unimaginable. When they met, the large woman took Evka's face gently in her hands and kissed her. And Evka threw her arms around her and kissed her back!

Stunned, all he could do was watch helplessly as the scene unfolded. The two women, totally focused on each other, arms entwined, mounted the steps, and walked into the restaurant together. It was another ten minutes before he could pull himself out of his stupor to start the car.

Obviously, this changed everything.

A one-night fling was one thing, he could forgive that. He had forgiven that! But this, this was something else. This was so ugly . . . so wrong. How could Evka have done this? And how had he not seen it coming? How could he ever have been attracted to a woman capable of such an abomination?

He slammed his car into gear. Every fiber of his body wanted to stomp on the gas and peel out of the parking lot, but he maintained control. This was not the end. No female was going to make a fool out of him.

Without consciously deciding to, he turned north onto I-5 instead of going home. Tonight would be a Portland night. Then he would think this through. And make a plan.

4

After he left the restaurant and saw what he couldn't unsee, he bolted to Portland, barely staying within the speed limit. Once in town, he oozed his truck down a familiar, darkened street in Old Town. His usual, Cherry, was standing with some friends, cigarette in one hand, rubbing her upper arms to stay warm. He pulled over to the curb. Pasting a smile on her face, she started walking toward the car, giving him that look, but at the last minute, he sped up and kept going.

Tonight he wanted something else. Something more.

He wasn't sure where to find what he wanted, so he just kept cruising until he got to a darker street, less busy. Hookers on this street weren't the freshest fruit on the tree. More like old, wrinkled apples that had fallen on the ground. And as far as he could tell, no pimps to protect them.

He slowed down to a smooth crawl, anticipation building, looking them over as he cruised past, trying to select the right one. At the end of the street, he turned around and made another pass. This time, he slowed to a stop in front of a saggy-faced, scrawny woman in a hot pink miniskirt, black lace bra, torn fishnet stockings, and high-heeled, white boots. Classic. Her exposed midriff displayed several rolls of pale, dimpled fat.

The only thing she had in common with Evka was dark hair.

He didn't bother with a hotel. The fury that had been building surged so brutally, he just took her around the corner in the alley for twenty bucks. She said her name was Raven. Raven did what even Cherry wouldn't, but in the end, even she screamed.

Once.

If anyone heard, no one came running. Zipping his pants and tossing his condom to join its many friends littering the ground, he shoved Raven's crumpled body behind a dumpster. Then he went home, scoured himself clean, and got into bed. He slept for a few hours, then lay awake, staring at the ceiling.

At six a.m. he went to Mass. Saturday morning Mass was a calming ritual and so deeply ingrained, he never missed it. After his father died, Saturday mornings were the only time his mother didn't have to work. Most of his childhood, she held down two or three jobs. Those precious few hours were their special time together.

He didn't keep cooking supplies at this place, so when he was in Portland, he ate out, mostly at a small diner around the corner and just a couple of blocks away from the church. He stopped there for breakfast after Mass, then spent the rest of the Sabbath sitting in his apartment, staring out the window at the rain, giving his brain free rein.

He already knew what he wanted to do. There was only one suitable response to Evka's betrayal. He just had to decide how—and when—to do it.

His brain clicked through all the options, mentally exploring various scenarios, keeping what worked, discarding the rest. It was like a giant chess game. It was a pity no one would ever record the moves or celebrate his victory. Everyone had always underestimated him.

Unless he wanted to get arrested or spend the rest of his life on the run, he needed to make Evka's death look like natural causes. It had to be something that worked fast and would be undetectable.

IN PLAIN SIGHT

A smile spread across his face but didn't reach his eyes. He knew just the thing. It would take precise planning. He would have to wait for just the right time and circumstances to use it. It would require patience, but he could do that. Patience was his strong suit.

He ran through the plan in his mind one last time, decided it was viable. Now he just needed to execute it. He leaned back in his chair and steepled his hands, staring out over the street without focusing on anything or anyone in particular.

The drug he needed was readily available at the center, of course. The beauty of injecting Evka with a drug from her own pharmaceutical stock was sweet, but all of those substances were tightly controlled. Locked up securely and no way to sneak any here, or even steal small amounts over time. Evka would notice. No, stealing any amount would be detected. He'd have to find another way.

But he had a source. He normally only bought two street drugs from him, MDMA and rohypnol, otherwise known as Ecstasy and roofies—for the times he talked a waitress and not a hooker into coming with him to a hotel room—but his dealer was always bragging he could get him anything he wanted. Claimed he had those kinds of connections.

There was always a junkie who needed a fix, he said. And some of those junkies worked in hospitals, pharmacies, or for shipping companies. He could get him anything he wanted. It just might take some time. Before Christmas, he promised.

They communicated via text. The number changed frequently, so he assumed the guy used burner phones. Hopefully, the most recent number he had was still good.

5

MONDAY, JANUARY 3

EUGENE, OREGON

The blinding sun glinting off the cars in the parking lot was deceptive.

Logan zipped her coat up to her chin and went back in for gloves. While she was there, she rummaged a little deeper in the basket by the door and grabbed the warm, wool beanie Amy got her for Christmas. Given the recent windfall from the music video, Logan insisted she didn't need anything, but everyone said it wasn't Christmas without gifts, and she did love the hat. It was a pretty heather color and soft.

She checked herself in the hall mirror to make sure she had everything. Waterproof Timberlands, old jeans, long-sleeve t-shirt, hoodie, coat—gloves and hat. She'd been warned that some of the residents where she was going were allowed to wander the grounds and often peed and pooped on themselves at will, so not to wear anything she couldn't hose off. Today was Logan's first day of training for her new volunteer position at the Cascades Raptor Center. They said the worst offender for defecation crimes was Lethe, the turkey vulture.

Her shift started at 8:00 a.m. Since she was housesitting Jean's rental, she only had a fifteen-minute drive. Several contractors were coming to do work on the rental this week, but none of them were scheduled for today.

It was a long story, but basically, it was her grandson's fault that Logan had decided to volunteer at the Cascades Raptor Center. During a visit to the Orange Coast Aquarium in Newport over the holidays, four-year-old Ian had fallen in love with one of their animal ambassadors, a great horned owl named Opa. The young man putting Opa through her paces was engaging and knowledgeable. When the beautiful owl spread her wings at the end of the demonstration, it was all over. Ian was hooked, as was everyone else.

Ever since, Ian wanted anything and everything owl, from a stuffed Hedwig to owl sheets to picture books. *Owl Moon, A Little Owl on a Big Adventure,* and *Little Owl's Night.*

He wasn't the only one. Logan had spotted one or two of the enigmatic raptors in the forest behind her house, perched in a tree or doing fly-bys in the yard, and was fascinated with them herself. When she'd gone onto the Cascades Raptor Center's website to plan a visit for Ian the next time they were in town, she stumbled onto their volunteer page. Since it only required a commitment of one day a week, she filled out the application and hit send.

She was still getting used to having the luxury of time to do things like this. With Tilly handling Fractals so well, Logan found herself spending more time composing music and playing Bella. She had decided not to make any definite plans, but to follow her passions as they came.

They told her there were five volunteer areas. Greeters worked mainly in the gift shop and collected entrance fees,

IN PLAIN SIGHT

Facilities people kept the grounds in good shape, built enclosures, and required skills Logan did not have. She qualified to be a docent, which would have been fun, but then she wouldn't get to work directly with the animals. Logan much preferred to work behind the scenes.

In the end, it was a toss-up between Resident Care and Wildlife Hospital Team. She would have been happy with either assignment, but because she and Amy had rescued a baby sea otter one summer and helped in its rehabilitation, she'd been assigned to work with the vet as a member of the Wildlife Hospital Team.

Checking her backpack for water and snacks before she pulled out of the parking lot, Logan aimed the car south. Volunteers only worked half days, so she didn't need to pack a lunch. She'd grab something on the way home.

Following her GPS, she wound her way through an increasingly forested residential area, gaining in elevation as she went. She was just about to give the center a call to make sure she was on the right road, when she saw a small sign nailed to a tree. She turned in and pulled up the steep, gravel drive just as a tall, rangy man was opening the gate. He waved her in and showed her where to park.

"You must be Logan," he said.

Faded blue eyes smiled down at her out of a deeply lined face, topped by a frayed baseball cap. A tucked in, long sleeve chambray shirt, worn work pants and scuffed boots completed his ensemble. Opening the car door, he held out his hand to help her out.

Not needing any help, but not wanting to offend the man, Logan extended her own like a debutante and allowed the gentlemanly gesture. With a trace of a southern drawl, he introduced himself as Jimmy and said he'd be taking her back to meet the vet. His whole nature was unrushed and kind. She liked him instantly.

Logan tried to take everything in as they went. First came the gift shop and what she assumed must be offices, then a scattering of one-story, wooden buildings and large, open-wire aviaries connected by meandering, uneven paths. Signs outside each enclosure told you what kind of raptor was inside. Bald eagle, barred owl, peregrine falcon . . . some kind of hawk . . . she couldn't read the signs fast enough and still keep up with Jimmy's long legs. When they arrived, she looked back over her shoulder. She would definitely need a map to find her car at the end of her shift.

"Here you go, Doc," Jimmy said as they entered the animal clinic. "I've got your new helper."

"In here, Jimmy!" a woman's slightly accented voice called out. Logan remembered from the vet's bio on the website that she was from the Czech Republic originally.

Jimmy led her back to a small, windowless, white-tiled room with a drain in the middle of the floor. Deep shelves, topped with large airline kennels were arranged all along the edges. A slight woman with a glossy, chestnut braid halfway down her back was gently placing a large raptor of some kind back inside. Once the bird settled, she pulled a cover over the top, making sure it covered all the sides as well. She stripped off her gloves and went to the sink to wash her hands.

"Hello!" she said. "Just put her in my office, Jimmy, I'll be right there."

Later, the vet explained there were very strict rules about who was allowed to interact with the injured raptors in the medical side of things. Until she was trained, Logan would be working in other areas. One of those areas, she would learn later that morning, was in the backyard behind the clinic, hosing out raptor kennels.

After getting Logan situated in the office with a cup of coffee, Jimmy left to attend to whatever other duties he had. A few minutes later, the vet came in and sat down, picking up and scanning what looked like a printout of her application on her desk. Friendly, but brisk, she got right to the point.

"I'm Evka, nice to meet you," she said. "It looks like you have prior experience in this type of setting, which should give you a leg up, but raptors are very different from sea otters. You will have a lot to learn. Today you'll be shadowing Neil. He's one of our trainers. Neil's been here longer than any of us except Louise, I think. He should be able to answer any questions you have."

Logan knew from her interview that Louise was the founder and director of the center. She also noted from the staff bios online that Evka was Evka Novotna. She received her degree and initial training in Australia, worked several places there, and then was in charge of a large animal hospital at a well-known game park in Kenya. She'd come to the Cascades Raptor Center two years ago. Logan wondered what drew her to this less prestigious assignment. Maybe she just liked Oregon. Wanted some cool green after all that heat and sun in Africa.

". . . You'll start with the food station, weigh ins. Are you squeamish, Logan?" she asked, pinning Logan with a direct gaze. "The raptors eat fresh meat."

6

The raptors did indeed eat fresh meat. Rabbit, quail, fish . . . Following the precise instructions given to her by Neil, Logan hacked them up, placing the delectable treats—with the fur, scales, bloody bones and all—onto plastic trays, according to the needs and preferences of each raptor. The eagle got a rabbit leg today. When asked why the raptors couldn't just eat hamburger, Neil explained they needed the nutrients and roughage provided by the whole animal. Made sense.

Gloved and masked, with her hair pulled back in a braid not nearly as neat as Evka's, with a lunch-lady hairnet, Logan had no desire to take a selfie. She'd promised Ben she'd document her first day, but it would be a cold day in hell before he saw her like this, up to her elbows in animal carrion. This was not a glamour job.

Propped up in front of her workstation was a whiteboard with an indecipherable grid of words and numbers. Neil translated the shorthand. BAEA 21-34 indicated a bald eagle, log number 34 that came in 2021. The raptor's name, Atticus, was followed by the grams of food to be fed that day and his weight in grams. Atticus weighed 4815 grams or about 10.5 pounds.

Only the resident raptors had names. Everyone hoped recently rescued raptors would be released back into the wild.

As they worked, Logan observed her guide. Somewhere in his early sixties she guessed, he looked like any other man you might see out mowing his lawn on a Saturday morning. Thick body, round shouldered, a small set of love handles bulged over his belted khaki pants. His hair was thinning and streaked with gray, but he still had a full moustache. He'd probably been a blonde at some point as his skin was fair. His side-parted, neatly combed hair was frozen in a conservative style he probably hadn't changed since high school.

Logan looked down at her work so he wouldn't see her smile. Vanity revealed. The man used hair spray.

While they finished divvying up the goodies and handing them off to other staff and volunteers to deliver, Aaron, the young man who had so impressed Ian with his great horned owl wrangling, came in and pulled up a stool. She wondered if he still took Opa out to the Orange Coast Aquarium in Newport for animal ambassador demonstrations.

Neil glowered at him. Aaron ignored him and swiveled to face Logan.

"They've got you doing the fun stuff right away, I see," Aaron said, smiling up at her with even, white teeth.

About Logan's height and on the slender side, Aaron balanced easily on the stool, even leaning back a little. Dark hair curled at the collar of his forest green staff shirt. He wore his untucked over his jeans.

Aaron immediately put Logan in mind of her late husband, Jack. An attractive man who knew it.

He ran his fingers through his longish hair before replacing his ball cap. This practiced move probably had a predictable effect on most women, but after Jack, Logan was immune.

Besides, she was probably fifteen years Aaron's senior. He had much younger game around to hunt. Knowing his type, she assumed the man enjoyed the hunt more than the catch.

Logan laughed, finished peeling off her gloves and deposited them along with the hair net in the stainless-steel trash can near the sink.

"Yep, our Neil knows how to show the ladies a good time," Aaron said. "But, not as good as me. I've got you next," he said, giving her a wink.

Inwardly, Logan rolled her eyes.

"Follow me!" he said, not waiting for her response. Exiting the kitchen, he did a fairly good Pied Piper imitation.

Logan turned to Neil to see if there was anything else he needed her to do, but he had already turned his back on them, entering the morning's data into his computer.

Aaron's part of the training, Logan had to admit, was more fun. Over the next hour, he introduced her to what seemed like each and every one of the almost forty raptors residing in the areas open to the public. Eagles, hawks, falcons, kestrels, turkey vultures, and several kinds of owls. A bright and funny tour guide, Aaron knew their names, their quirks, and had an endless store of anecdotes and avian facts. After a while, she stopped taking notes and just enjoyed the stories. In spite of herself, he was growing on her. Maybe she'd misjudged him.

When they got to Opa's aviary, Logan told him about seeing both of them at the Aquarium in Newport over Christmas and how much Ian had enjoyed his presentation. It was a shame he couldn't be here to see Opa again. Her grandson lived in California and wouldn't be back up for a visit for a while.

"Well, we'd better do something about that," Aaron said, reaching for the yellow pad of paper Logan brought to take notes on. He scribbled something on a blank page with a Sharpie he had in one of his myriad pockets, then tore it off and handed the pad back to Logan.

7

Entering the aviary, Aaron coaxed Opa onto her weigh station first, and then onto his gloved arm with a bit of fresh meat from a pouch on his belt. When she settled, he angled toward Logan and held the paper up in front of his chest and flashed a brilliant smile along with his message.

Hi, Ian! Come Visit Me Soon! Opa

While Aaron mugged for the camera, Logan snapped several shots with her phone. Ian was going to love this!

At the end of his guided tour, Aaron deposited Logan in the before-mentioned backyard area, where a bubbly blonde named Chrissie was lining up the kennels that needed to be cleaned out.

Logan remembered her from orientation. Chrissie had started at the center as a volunteer in high school but was now employed part time as a resident care assistant while she lived at home and attended the community college nearby. Whether it was because her grades weren't good enough to get her into U of O, or to save money on tuition or dorm rooms, Logan didn't know.

For the next hour, as they worked in tandem, Chrissie's idealism and passion poured out in a steady stream of chatter, her curly blond hair bobbing with each emphatic statement. It was both heartening and cringeworthy at the same time. To Chrissie's young eyes, no matter the topic, the world was black and white. And she wasn't afraid to proselytize.

"Everyone should give up cars and airplanes and meat to save the planet!

"At least half of all privately held land should be turned into wildlife sanctuaries.

"Everyone has a one and only soul mate and no one should settle for less!"

These were just a few of Chrissie's firmly stated opinions.

Maybe it was being raised by her father, but Logan had never worn her feelings on her sleeve quite like Chrissie did. During the director's talk at orientation, when she wasn't tearing up over lost habitat, greedy corporations, and thoughtless, human incursions into raptor territory, Chrissie gazed longingly at Aaron from across the room. Since Aaron didn't reciprocate, or even seem to notice Chrissie's existence, it was painful to watch. What was worse, Aaron seemed to be casting glances Evka's way.

Logan wished she could help the poor girl see he just wasn't into her, but she wasn't her mother. This may just be a lesson she would have to learn for herself.

Today, Logan focused on her own lesson in how to adjust the hose nozzle to avoid getting raptor shit all over herself when it splattered everywhere. As it was, when she got back to her car, she wished she'd thought to bring an old beach towel to drape over the seat. Living half a block from the ocean in Jasper, she always had one with her in California, but up here in Oregon, she'd gotten out of the habit.

That night, after a long, hot shower, she forwarded Opa's pictorial invitation to Amy to show Ian. Presidents Day was coming up in February. Amy organized school field trips for the Sea Otter Center, so she had that week off. Liam and Ben had a fishing trip planned, so she'd have to see if Amy wanted to bring Ian up for a little Oregon R&R.

Logan loved being a mom and grandma, but she was glad her daughter didn't need to live right next door. There was a lot to be said for having your own space. Amy and Logan were both McKenna women, and McKenna women came with strong, independent streaks.

They also came with a deep well of love, that when they decided to give it, gave it all. Friend or lover, when they let you in, you were in.

Speaking of lovers . . . Logan reached for her phone to call hers. Her new husband picked up on the first ring. She had been a little worried marriage would dampen their desire for each other, but if anything, it had heightened it. They were more playful and relaxed. Now that she fully trusted Ben, she felt herself free to let go and really enjoy the ride.

8

The next few weeks passed quickly. Tilly called and reminded her they had their annual meeting with the school board about *Fractals* in May, but that was a couple of months away. It was on her calendar, but for now, Logan was enjoying her new life up here in Oregon.

Things had settled into something of a routine. A routine not imposed from the outside but emerging from her natural rhythms. Having lived by the demands of business and motherhood for years, it was a luxury she did not take for granted.

She usually got in a run before enjoying her coffee and breakfast burrito at Pirate's. Wednesdays were Coffee Crew confabs with Sam and Jean. Home and showered by nine or ten, she'd compose or play until lunch, catch up on emails and Fractals business, do whatever errands she had and be back immersed in her music until it started to get dark.

When Ben wasn't here, dinner was usually Bayview Thai or Tidepools Pizza. She'd buy two or three entrees and eat off of those for a couple of days. Nothing wrong with green curry or pizza for breakfast. With a few apples in the bowl on the counter, she had most of the food groups covered.

Mondays were volunteer days at the raptor center, but occasionally, like today, a Wednesday, she'd fit in an extra shift. Evka had called last night and said they got in two new rescues yesterday, a barn owl with a damaged wing and a juvenile red-tailed hawk that had been struck by a car that was pretty bad off. Neil, who often helped her with difficult cases, was off this week for his annual vacation and she could use the extra hands if Logan was available.

Taking her coffee to go and skipping her run, Logan was on the road by five-thirty in order to get there by eight. She let Evka know she could stay late if she needed her. She'd promised Jean she'd go up and check on the remodel of her rental this week, anyway, so she wouldn't have to drive back to Depoe Bay tonight. Not knowing how long she'd need to be in Eugene, she packed a bag and made sure Bella was secure in her violin case and tucked safely into the back seat.

When she arrived at the center, Jimmy already had the gate open and was spreading a pile of bark chip on one of the side berms. Before she walked back to the clinic, she handed him a sticky pecan roll from Pirate's. Logan had discovered he was a big fan of any and all sweets. Jimmy tipped his hat in thanks and shambled off to the open-air tool shed that constituted his office.

When Logan arrived, Evka was already swamped. Logan quickly put her gear away and began washing her hands.

"Where do you want me?" she asked.

She and Evka had developed something of a shorthand working together over the last couple of months. Logan admired the vet's calm, yet compassionate, efficiency in dealing with the usually terrified birds. Other than deer and rabbits, she had learned that raptors are some of the most sensitive and skittish animals. A wild raptor will often throw itself repeatedly against the wire boundaries of its enclosure until it dies, rather than succumb to the attentions of humans. This made them particularly difficult and dangerous to help.

But Evka had a way with them. As did Aaron. Logan had seen them work together many times, somehow managing to calm the fiercely beautiful wild creatures—at least for a few seconds—so they could get them into a kennel or onto a table so they could treat them.

After their charges had received breakfast and medicines and had their wounds attended to, Evka and Logan covered the kennels, darkened the room, and took a break.

"You want some?" Evka asked after filling her own mug with coffee that had been warming in the pot next to her desk for several hours.

"Sure," Logan said.

Evka handed her a red one she lifted down from a mug tree on the counter. Logan added cream and sugar when she got it, although she usually liked it black. This brew needed some mellowing.

Evka sank into her chair, closed her eyes, and sipped.

"Were you up all night?" Logan asked.

"Mostly," Evka said.

Chrissie walked in. As a member of the Resident Care Team who helped supervise volunteers for that group, she'd been busy until now picking up the remainder of the raptors' breakfasts and cleaning the aviaries.

From what Logan had gleaned, Chrissie wanted to be a trainer. She was taking classes at the local community college and had put in her hours as a volunteer, but now, even though she worked part time at the center, she wasn't advancing as fast as she wanted or thought she deserved. The girl was obviously chaffing at the bit for more responsibility.

"Need any help?" she asked Evka, ignoring Logan.

"No, we're good, Chrissie," Evka said. "Thank you."

When Evka didn't elaborate, Chrissie left.

One of their patients, the severely injured red-tailed hawk, had required surgery. For one brief instant, when she was helping Evka transfer him to one of the airline kennels, the hawk looked directly at her. The depth of fierce intelligence in his eyes made a strong, visceral impact on Logan. Right then, she committed to doing everything in her power to make sure this beautiful, intelligent wild animal survived.

As the day wore on, they had another new rescue intake. Not a raptor, but a great blue heron that had inadvertently hitched a ride on a semi and wound up with a broken beak and damaged left eye. By 4:00 p.m., Evka looked exhausted. Logan was tired, too, but she hadn't been up all night and didn't carry the full responsibility of each animal's survival. Evka had and did.

And Logan knew the red-tailed hawk could not be left alone. He would require at least one more night of twenty-four-hour surveillance until he was out of the woods.

"I'll be happy to spell you off and on tonight," Logan said. "I've slept in less comfortable chairs in airports back when we were doing software training for clients and flights got held up."

Evka smiled gratefully, "No, thanks. That is so nice of you to offer, Logan, but it is not necessary."

"I really don't mind, and I've already packed a bag. I'm checking on a friend's rental property over near the university, anyway. I can help you tonight, then crash at her place tomorrow."

"Well, if you are serious, I could use the help. Normally, I wouldn't risk transferring the red tail, but he is stable, and I won't do this guy much good without some sleep," she said. "That said, camping out won't be necessary. I have an extra bedroom you can use."

"Well then, consider yourself saddled with two extra house guests tonight," Logan said. "What do you want to do for dinner? Is there a place on the way we can drive through?"

9

Evka pulled out several takeout menus from her desk drawer. "Take your pick," she said. "These places are all close. I like everything, so order whatever you want. We'll pick it up on the way home. The least I can do is buy you dinner. It won't take long to load the Outback. Tell them we can be there in fifteen or twenty minutes."

A menu from a place called Athena's caught Logan's eye. It had been a while since she had Greek food. The coast had some great restaurants, but not the kind of variety you found inland.

As usual, Logan overordered. The enticing aroma of gyros, moussaka, avgolemono, Greek salad, and baklava almost made them pull over to the side of the road and dig in right there. But Logan sat on her hands and Evka kept her hands on the wheel, so they made it home without incident. Logan had no idea what the raptor in the rear of the vehicle thought about the foreign aromas wafting back to his kennel. Later, she would learn that hawks don't have a very active sense of smell, so the delicious food probably didn't make much of an impression.

A few minutes later, Evka turned onto Madronna and pulled into the gravel drive of an older, ranch style home. The front yard was neat if scrubby, with a few rhododendrons along the side. Tree tops rising behind the humble house hinted at some natural landscaping beyond.

"You're really close to my friend's place," Logan said as they got out. "She and her husband own a rental just north of here. On Longview. Her name is Jean. She's the one I'm doing the housesitting for. You'd like her. In fact, she might be coming up Friday to meet with the contractor. Maybe we can get together while she's here."

"I already have plans that night, but bring her over to the center Friday," Evka said. "We can give her the grand tour."

Logan handled the food, her bag and Bella, while Evka carefully carried in their patient and secured his kennel in a quiet back bedroom to the right of the front door. Another hallway led to the left. Evka indicated the bathroom was that way, along with her office and bedroom.

They'd left Logan's car locked up back at the center. Evka assured her it was safe, but with a cop for a brother, Logan had learned not to leave anything she didn't want to lose in her car, locked or not, so had brought her valuables with her.

Logan looked out the large picture window in the dining room and nodded appreciatively. Thick-trunked evergreens filled the view.

"Nice!" Logan said.

"Yes, that's my solace," said Evka, joining Logan at the table with a roll of paper towels and some utensils. "I picked this house because it's right on the southern edge of Hendrick's Park. Eighty-acres of woods and trails. And only ten minutes from work."

Logan understood the appeal. That was one of the big selling points for her own home in Depoe Bay. It backed up onto forestry land and at least for the foreseeable future, would never be built on. Logan spent a lot of time on the back deck, enjoying the peaceful quiet.

Unnoticed by the two women as they polished off the majority of their haul from Athena's, an ivory quarter moon rose over the crooked tip of a two-hundred-year-old Douglas fir, silhouetting it softly against the flat, slate sky. Evka opened a buttery chardonnay to accompany their meal.

All Logan wanted to do was take a nap, but she rallied when she remembered that the vet had been up for almost two days straight.

When Evka started to clean up, Logan shook her head and said, "You go get some shuteye, I'll take first watch."

Evka didn't argue but gave her instructions for the hawk and made Logan promise to wake her up in four hours—sooner if she needed anything.

Logan reassured her she was fine. Once Evka finally went to her room, Logan used the bathroom, cleaned up the kitchen, then wandered into the living room to find a comfortable, but not too comfortable, place to sit and read. She didn't want to fall asleep on the job.

Expecting the fireplace to need real logs and wondering if Evka had any and where they were, Logan was relieved to discover it was a gas fireplace and easily lit with the turn of a key on the left side, just above the baseboard.

Digging into her bag, she retrieved her kindle and cell phone charger, then settled onto the couch with a blanket Evka got her from the hall closet. She apologized for not having more but said the guest bedroom was pretty warm and there was another one on the bed in there.

"Good night, Evka!" Logan said firmly, "I'm fine, really. Go to bed!"

There was another glass of wine left in the bottle, but afraid of nodding off in front of the warm fire, Logan made herself some hot tea instead.

By midnight, she was deep into 1922 post-revolutionary Russia, keeping company with a former aristocrat under house arrest in a luxury hotel. Amor Towles had only written three books she knew of, and she adored every one of them. This was her third reading of *A Gentleman in Moscow*.

Just as Count Rostov was removing something hidden in the legs of one of his finer pieces of furniture, a key turned in the lock of Evka's front door. Logan was so absorbed in the story she hadn't heard anyone drive up.

Who would be coming in this late at night? As far as she knew, Evka didn't have any family here and she hadn't mentioned anything about roommates.

Logan also noticed that, typical of Oregon, the weather had changed while she was curled up with a good book. She heard rain possibly mixed with hail beating against the windows, when a gust of wind flung open the door, sending a flurry of dead leaves skittering across the entryway, followed by a very large woman.

When she saw Logan, the woman—a big, blonde bruiser dressed all in black, studded motorcycle leather—did not look happy.

10

"Who are you?" she demanded.

Almost as wide as she was tall, Logan imagined the woman either worked as a bouncer at a bar or captained a roller derby team.

"I'm Logan. Who are you?" she said, trying to keep her voice from shaking.

She wasn't about to let this woman intimidate her. Obviously, it was someone Evka knew—she had a key. But it was also pretty obvious Evka hadn't been expecting her.

Instead of answering Logan's question, the roller derby queen demanded, "Where's Evka?"

When Logan didn't immediately answer, she gave her an 'I'll-deal-with-you-later' look and strode down the hall toward Evka's bedroom. If she had been in her way, Logan was sure she would have shoved her aside.

"Evka!" she bellowed.

Physically half the size of this woman, Logan did not try to stop her. She'd be shaken off like a fly. Instead, she grabbed her phone, which she'd left on the charger. Black screen.

Damn!

She heard her barge into Evka's bedroom and slam the door shut behind her. This was followed by some shouting, then urgent, quiet arguing.

Definitely someone Evka knows.

She'd just have to wait until they came out to find out what was going on. With nothing else to do for now, Logan checked on the red tail. Not her house. Not her business.

If the noise had bothered the injured animal, he had since settled down. He seemed fine.

When she returned to the living room, a chastened-looking Evka was leaning against the back of the couch. Her unexpected guest stood defiantly next to her, arms folded, jaw set, glaring at Logan.

"I am sorry," Evka said to Logan. "I wasn't expecting Mia tonight."

"Obviously," Mia said, through gritted teeth.

The vet attempted to keep the thin veneer of civil conversation going.

"Mia, this is Logan . . . Logan McKenna, one of our new volunteers. She's helping me tonight with a raptor I needed to bring home."

Mia continued to glare, the only change in her expression a narrowing of laser blue eyes with new suspicion.

Evka soldiered on. "Logan, this is Mia, she . . . we knew each other in Kenya, from the animal hospital. Mia is a wildlife biologist."

As if that explains anything.

Mia wasn't happy with her introduction either.

"You can't even *say* it?! I thought we were past all that, that *you* were past all that!" she growled, slamming her key down onto the small, entryway table on her way out. "When you figure out what to call me, what I mean to you, and what *she* means to you, let me know, Evka."

IN PLAIN SIGHT

Logan expected an emphatic bang of a slammed door to punctuate her exit, but the soft click of the lock was somehow almost louder . . . and full of tender pain.

"I am so sorry," Evka whispered, slumped against the back of the couch.

Logan had never seen the confident woman like this. It was like someone let the air out of her. Then, pulling herself together, she rubbed her face briskly and went into the kitchen. She returned with a bottle of Elijah Craig and two short glasses. "I don't think wine will do the trick," she said.

Logan accepted a generous pour and they both sat down on the couch. Evka got up to turn up the gas fireplace. Logan let her take her time.

Finally, she said, "I should have told you about Mia. You deserve an explanation."

"Your private business is your business, Evka," Logan said. "You don't owe me anything."

"Mia and I met in Kenya. I ran the hospital there and Mia worked with the park rangers. As I said, she's a wildlife biologist. She was also doing research on sable antelope. There are only about fifty of them left in the wild. And she helped me with injured animals within the park. I don't know how she does what she does. She's not afraid of anything. I mean, a lion was waking up a little early once from anesthesia, but she just kept on taking measurements! Barely got out of there with her skin."

She took a thoughtful pull of her whiskey and stared into the fire. Logan waited for her to continue.

"It will make more sense if I start from the beginning. I was married—before," Evka said. "To a man named Tim Bancroft. Tim and I were in the same cohort at the University of Sydney. We were best friends. He followed me to Kenya, we married there. It seemed right at the time.

"But Africa did not suit Tim. Neither did I, apparently. He returned to Australia and we divorced. Overall, it was very civil. We agreed to terms over the phone. I was kind of in a daze back then, gave him everything he asked for. He sent me the papers, and I signed them and sent them back. I thought we were normal, but I had nothing to compare it to. When he left, I felt more relief than sadness.

"But when Mia arrived at the park a few months later, I took one look at her and felt what I can only describe as an electric jolt. Unlike with Tim, we did not start as friends. It was all . . . so much more! I'd never felt such strong emotions. We quickly became lovers, but just as quickly, began fighting. I broke it off several times and finally decided the only way I was going to figure things out was to leave—to be alone for a while. When this job came up, I took it."

"So what happened?" Logan asked. "Did you decide you wanted to be with Mia after all? Did you ask her to come here?"

"No, Mia did that on her own. Last fall, she completed her work at the park and got accepted to the Hatfield Marine Science Center in Newport on the coast. Not far from where you live, actually. She joined a twelve-month stranded marine mammals research group. That gave us a year to figure things out. We've been seeing each other off and on—mostly on, for the last few months, but in secret. That was on my insistence. Just until I figured things out."

"Did you know she was coming?" Logan asked.

"No, I did not," Evka said. "Mia can be very insistent. And it is flattering to have someone uproot their life and move halfway across the world for you. But I still haven't decided if that's the life I want. I'm not even sure I'm gay or what that means, really. Maybe I'm bi. I had a normal married life, or thought I did, until Mia came along."

"Had you had other relationships before?" Logan asked. "With women, I mean."

"No, I hadn't had any relationships of any kind before Tim. I was too busy working and going to school," she said. "Mia says she has always known she's gay and thinks I'm just afraid to come out of the closet, but I don't think that's it. I've been attracted to men, too, since then, so I know I can feel both."

"What I can't explain is that since I came here, other than a very brief drunken mistake when I first arrived, and until Mia arrived, I have been happy not being with anyone. I don't think everyone is meant to be married or paired or whatever. But as always, Mia is an overpowering presence. I don't think clearly when she's around. Now I feel confused again."

Logan's first instinct was to advise Evka to tell Mia to get lost—at least until she knew if that's what she wanted, but kept her mouth shut. Unsolicited advice was rarely taken. And who was she to judge? After Jack's betrayal, it had taken her several years to learn to trust a man. She finally accepted Ben's love for her and realized getting married didn't mean giving up her new independence and sense of self.

"And, as you saw tonight, Mia is quick to make assumptions," said Evka. "I'll make it very clear to her tomorrow that you and I are simply good friends and work colleagues."

Logan agreed that would be an excellent idea. The thought of Mia slashing her tires or worse because she thought she and Evka were involved in any romantic way scared her shitless.

11

Since she was already up, Evka took the next hawk-sitting shift and Logan went gratefully to bed. Her guest bedroom was across the hall from Evka's with a small window looking out onto the front yard. She left the blinds open a sliver and the nightstand lamp on. If Mia decided to return to make her point more emphatically, Logan wanted to make sure it was obvious she was not in Evka's room. She dropped into a deep sleep immediately and didn't wake until she smelled coffee.

Following the aroma of French roast into the kitchen, she saw breakfast already on the table and Evka looking rested and with an underlying energy. Logan was pleased to see her friend in a good place. She must have come to some kind of decision last night, because her movements seemed fueled by an inner resolve and excitement.

Over baklava and French roast, Evka said the red tail was doing so well she'd gone back to bed herself for a few hours. She again apologized for last night's unpleasantness and promised she would talk with Mia.

"Thank you for being such a good listener, Logan," Evka said. "It really helped."

"No problem, Evka," Logan said. "Next time Ben and I get in a fight, I'll be calling you!"

Evka laughed. Logan and Ben didn't fight much, but she didn't want the vet to feel like the only one with relationship problems. She liked Evka and didn't want there to be any awkwardness between them.

On the way back to the center, Evka reminded Logan to bring her friend out for a tour Friday. She said she would.

*****

Traffic was light and she pulled into the garage at Jean's rental house in plenty of time to accept delivery of the new gas stove. It was supposed to arrive sometime between ten and four.

An old Craftsman, the two-bedroom-plus-office house gleamed with lots of dark wood and windows that overlooked an easy-to-maintain yard. It would be rented to visiting faculty or grad students and neither had much time for gardening. Jean and her husband had replaced all the appliances, but there still wasn't room for a dishwasher in the tiny kitchen. Logan didn't mind, she didn't have one in her 1940s fixer upper in Jasper, either.

Jean called and said unless she was called out for medical examiner duties, she would be there in time for dinner.

"Thompson's Steak House, okay?" she asked.

"If they have a ribeye medium rare with horseradish and a crispy-skinned baked potato with the works, and salad on the side, I'm in!" Logan said.

Jean laughed and got back to her patients.

The stove was delivered and installed by one o'clock. Jean kept emergency supplies of canned soup in the cupboard and a bowl of apples in the fridge, so Logan made herself lunch before falling asleep on the couch in front of the fire. She'd intended to work on her latest composition, but after last night's excitement and only a few hours' sleep, her eyelids drifted closed and stayed that way until Jean arrived.

Thompson's turned out to be a winner. Logan ordered her dream meal, Jean had filet mignon with a shrimp salad, and they shared a bottle of mineral water. Since she'd practically had whiskey for breakfast, Logan figured her liver could use the break.

Focusing on her meal, Logan let Jean take the lead in the conversation. She didn't think Evka would want her sharing her personal business. She did mention the extended invitation to take a tour and Jean welcomed the idea.

When they got back home, Logan got a text from Sam telling her she had wrapped up her story, so if the invitation was still open, she could drive up tomorrow and stay the weekend.

"Tell her about the Cascades Raptor Center tour tomorrow—see if she can make it up early and come with us on the tour," Jean called from the hallway as she hung up her coat.

Logan zipped a text to Sam.

"No, she says she can't get here before eleven or twelve, so we'll just meet her back here," Logan said. "And she'll pick up lunch."

"Perfect," said Jean. "We can get groceries tomorrow after the tour."

Logan gave Evka a call to make sure the informal tour was still on and check on the hawk's progress.

"Our patient is hanging in there," Evka said. "He's not out of the woods, yet. I may stay here tonight. It just depends on how he does today."

Logan moved into mom mode.

"But you hardly got any sleep last night . . . ," she said.

"Don't worry, I took a nap this afternoon, I'm good," Evka said. Then she lowered her voice. "Oh, and I am going to have a talk with Mia."

Not wanting to say anything in front of Jean about Evka's personal life, Logan just confirmed the time, "Okay, see you tomorrow, then. Let me know if anything changes. We'll be there by 8:00 a.m. We'll catch up then."

She hoped Evka would understand.

12

Driving was usually relaxing—a warm, safe bubble where he could be alone. He enjoyed being alone. But Evka had ruined it!

Now, every time he got in the car, the image of Evka kissing Mia in the parking lot welled up and wouldn't go away. He'd taken a peek at her phone one day and learned the woman's name. It disgusted him, they disgusted him, but he didn't care about the other woman. She was obviously a lesbian. Mannish face, hulking body—ugly.

But Evka. His Evka was beautiful . . . and normal. At least she used to be. But she had somehow turned. She had rejected the true, pure love he offered. Or would have if she'd just waited.

He went over and over the last year in his mind. After Evka foolishly slept with that boy, she had not repeated her bad behavior, so redeemed herself somewhat in his mind. By all outward appearances, she was coming around to being her old self. She smiled at him the other day when he held open the door for her. He had learned exactly how she liked her coffee—two sugars, no cream—and although each had different responsibilities, when she did need him for something, they worked seamlessly together. Evka didn't talk much, either. He liked that. He had given her a lot of time and space to come around, to notice him. His worth. The pure love she'd been waiting for.

He didn't like people in general, but he could imagine making room in his life for one perfect woman.

But she never had come around. For a while he thought she'd at least stopped her perverse activities, but then he'd driven by her house and seen Mia's truck in the driveway. That made up his mind. He had to do it.

He'd been waiting for the perfect opportunity to tell her of his love, now he waited for the perfect time to punish her, to wash the earth clean of her.

And it had to be done without disturbing the life he'd built for himself. He'd watched all those crime shows on TV. That's where killers made their mistake, but he was smarter, better. So last year, just before Christmas, he bought the drug he needed and stashed it with his roofies and E in his apartment in Portland until he figured out how and when to use it.

Tonight, as he drove, a plan began to form. His eyes glittered as he saw it all unfold in his mind.

Yes, this might just work.

There was no need to act rashly. He had all the time in the world. He was going to Portland anyway, to spend a little quality time with Cherry. He'd pick up his supplies then. Later, he'd drive to Eugene and go directly to Evka's house, get the job done. Before she'd betrayed him, he used to park outside her house in the dark, just watching, hoping to catch a glimpse of her elegant body moving around the house inside, walking past a window. Even her shadow excited him. He knew where she hid her spare key.

He went through it all again and didn't see any flaws in his plan.

IN PLAIN SIGHT

He wished he could share his brilliant plan with someone, but there was no one to tell. Still, he sat up straighter, felt lighter. Why had he waited so long to do this? No matter, tonight was the night! And there was absolutely no way he could ever be connected with the murder he was about to commit.

13

Bright, yellow sunlight flowed into the dining room and spilled across the hardwood floor. Logan wanted to sit and enjoy the warmth of the sun on her back while she enjoyed her coffee, but since they had no leftovers and hadn't been to the store yet, Jean suggested a stop at Studio One Café on the way to the center. She said it was definitely worth the detour.

It was. Jean ordered a sensible vegetable omelet while Logan went for the Full Big Easy, complete with Cajun Hollandaise and a side of pepper bacon.

The service was great. Forty-five minutes later, an old pro now, Logan was pointing out the Cascades Raptor Center sign to Jean.

"Pull in here," she said. "It's just up this hill."

Jimmy must have known they were coming because the gate was already open. When they emerged from the car, a muted buzzing of a saw came from the direction of his work shed. From new enclosures to wooden ramps and railings, Jimmy was always building or fixing something.

Weaving her way confidently past the offices and gift shop, then through the aviaries, Logan arrived at her destination without getting lost once. She remembered how foreign all this was when Jimmy led her back here on her first day.

The animal hospital consisted of a cluster of six rooms all dedicated to treating and returning injured or orphaned raptors back to the wild whenever possible. It also served as an area to euthanize those that were too far gone to be helped.

A very small percentage—as little as 1 percent of those animals that survived—qualified to become animal ambassadors the public was privileged to view out front or as part of a wildlife zoo encounter. An open outdoor area mainly used for cleaning kennels separated the building from the public areas out front.

Logan crossed the yard and opened a plain, wooden door. There were no windows on this side of the building. The lights were on in the hallway.

"She's probably in her office," Logan said, stepping in. "It's in the back. She's always in early. Or she could have stayed over if she had a new patient. I don't know who's working today, but everyone else will start coming in around eight, eight fifteen. I'll introduce you when they get here."

Logan pointed out several rooms as they walked past. Ward 1 . . . Radiology . . . Lab . . . ward 2 is opposite Evka's office . . . ward 3 is on the other side . . ."

"How many raptors do they have in here at one time?" Jean asked.

"In here or in the whole center?" said Logan.

"Both, either," Jean said.

"Louise, the director—she's great, I'll take you over to meet her later—she said fall and winter are the least busy times. We've only had fifteen or twenty come through here since I started, but they tell me spring and summer get really busy. Baby season. And, of course, they have the resident birds. There are around forty of those," Logan said.

"And just one vet," Jean said.

IN PLAIN SIGHT

"Yeah," Logan said, "She's pretty amazing. Just watching her work—her fingers are like magic—she saves animals I thought for sure wouldn't make it. And she talks to them, calms them down. They respond to the sound of her voice really well. Louise says they were lucky to get her. She used to run a large animal hospital in Kenya. Made pretty good money, too."

Before Jean could ask why the vet took a lower-paying job to come to Oregon, they arrived.

Logan knocked lightly on the half-open door, pushing it open as she stepped in.

"Evka? . . ."

Instead of the vet's normally tidy office, what greeted them was a complete wreck. Logan stood there for a second, taking it all in.

"Wow," Jean said, looking over her shoulder.

Reference manuals and books were strewn around the room helter-skelter, leaving mostly empty bookshelves. Only a solitary blue mug remained on a dishtowel next to the sink. Someone had swiped everything off the desk, dumping it all onto the floor next to it. The whiteboard behind the desk still had Evka's notes on the current hospital occupants, but across the top someone had scrawled "Back Off, Bitch!" in red ink.

The pièce de résistance was the pile of dead mice in the center of Evka's desk. Still relatively fresh, the acrid smell of burnt coffee had covered up the growing rotten stench of death.

After checking behind the desk to make sure Evka wasn't laying there injured from an attack, Logan automatically flipped the switch off the coffeepot and headed into the hallway to find her. Jean followed.

They backtracked methodically through each room Logan had pointed out to Jean on the way in. Evka ran a tight ship. Logan knew because she cleaned those rooms. A place for everything and everything in its place. But everything looked in order.

Ward 2 across the hall was clean and empty. Same with radiology and the lab. Ward 1 housed a barred owl whose wing tip Evka had had to repair and a Cooper's hawk that Logan remembered had had an unpleasant encounter with an outdoor housecat. Both were silent in their covered kennels. All looked as it should, except the red tail was missing.

He certainly wasn't well enough to be released, but maybe he'd had a setback and Evka needed to go back in to fix something. They headed back down the hall to ward 3—the one room they hadn't checked yet. When they passed the office, the chaos within reminded Logan that whoever trashed it hadn't been quiet about it. The raptors must have gone nuts.

Surely Evka would have heard the noise if she had been in ward 3. Only a thin wall separated that room from the office. She couldn't imagine why she would, but Logan found herself hoping Evka had taken the hawk back to her home again. Somewhere safe —before a destructive fury swept through that small room, leaving dead mice and a cryptic message. "Back off."

Back off from what?

Taking a deep breath in a vain attempt to slow her racing heart, Logan stood outside ward 3. The door was closed. With a growing sense of dread, she turned the knob and pushed. It wouldn't open all the way. Before she could look behind the door to see what was blocking it, she froze.

Straight ahead, Evka lay sprawled on the floor, face up, arms flung out, one leg straight the other bent, her head turned slightly away from them. Above her on a table sat an empty kennel, door hung open. To the right there was a small rolling table, fresh gauze, scissors, her laptop, and a half-empty, green Cascades Raptor Center coffee mug with an image of an owl on it. There was no blood or violence.

Instinctively, Logan rushed in, flipped on the light switch, and lifted Evka's wrist to find a pulse, but it was cold. Jean, gently moving Logan out of the way, knelt down, placing her index and middle fingers on the side of Evka's neck, in the soft, hollow area just beside her windpipe. She shook her head once, then took out her phone and called 911.

While Jean was giving the dispatcher the information she required, the empty raptor kennel suddenly registered with Logan. Evka must have been working with the red tail when she collapsed. Where was he?

Logan looked around for the injured hawk, then remembered the door was hard to open. Not wanting to, but needing to know, she pulled it back. Her worst fears were confirmed. Two dark, glassy eyes stared out from a small, feathered head. The sooty, hooked beak was partially open. She had seen him use this fearsome weapon to tear into a rabbit haunch. Now it lay harmless on the tile floor.

One wing spread open, exposing his soft, pale underbelly. The wound Evka had so lovingly repaired gaped open and raw. She must have been in the middle of changing his bandage when whatever had happened, happened. If there had been a breeze, the short feathers would have ruffled in the wind.

It was hard to connect this lifeless corpse with the fierce, wildlife she had held close against her body just days ago, keeping him warm and still so Evka could treat him.

In a daze, she looked back at Evka. Two vibrant lives—gone, just like that.

What happened here?

14

Knowing other staff and volunteers would be arriving soon, Logan forced herself to turn away. She'd feel her feelings later. She really didn't want to leave the dead hawk on the floor, but she knew enough not to disturb what could be a crime scene.

Evka could have had a seizure or a stroke or a heart attack or died of some other unknown, but natural cause. And the raptor could have panicked and flown wildly around the room until it ran itself into the wall and died that way, but two dead bodies—one human and one avian—plus a vandalized office could add up to more than an accident. The police would want everything left alone until they could figure out what happened.

For now, Logan focused instead on what needed to be done—what Evka would want done. The resident raptors would need to be fed and the two hospital patients cared for. Logan could do most of it, but she'd need some help, and she needed to let Louise know what was going on. She hated being the bearer of bad news, but the director needed to be told what had happened.

Once Louise recovered from the initial shock of the news that her vet was dead, she took charge. Her calm, commanding voice ran through the options. Since Neil was on vacation, she and Logan would need to handle the immediate needs of the animals—at least for today. Normally, Aaron would help, but he'd had a wisdom tooth extraction yesterday. If all went well, he'd be back Monday. Not a good time to be short-handed, but she could always call one of the trainers if they really needed help.

Logan could hear Louise dressing as they spoke. She said she would be there as soon as she could and would make some calls on the way. They needed to get another vet in here to check on the two recuperating raptors and any new emergencies as soon as possible. She asked Logan to have Jimmy secure the grounds and guide the police to the animal hospital if they got there before she did. Logan said she would.

Before she got off the phone, Louise asked, "You okay?"

"Yes, I'm fine," Logan said. "We'll be fine until you get here. Drive safe."

Something about the scene she'd just witnessed seemed off, but right now she couldn't pinpoint what it was. She'd have to go through it in her mind, later. Maybe when she relayed the events of the day to Ben in tonight's phone call, it would come to her.

*****

Jean told the dispatcher she would stay with the body until the police arrived. As a Medical Examiner herself, she knew to keep everyone out and not touch anything. When it was determined the Lane County ME was out on another call and would not be able to arrive at this location for several hours, Jean agreed to do the initial exam and take charge of the scene.

She had Logan lock the employee entrance door in the back at the end of the hallway.

Following Louise's instructions, Logan found some paper, a sharpie, and some scotch tape in the lab, then went back and taped a sign on the outside of the door, instructing arriving staff and volunteers to return to their homes until someone contacted them. Any training or cleanup the volunteers would have done could wait until the police released the scene. After the fact, she wished she'd thought to put on some exam gloves but remembered in time not to touch anything in Evka's office or ward 3. They'd probably already smudged whatever finger-prints might be on the exterior door when they came in.

When that was done, Logan went to find Jimmy. He was still in the work shed, sanding a long, two-by-six piece of cedar. He looked up and smiled when he saw her in the doorway.

"Good morning, Miss Logan. Louise will be happy I'm finally getting this one done," he said, running his hand across the surface of the board, squinting his eyes down the length of it. "Somebody used pine for that gift shop porch railing, and it's been rotting out." Satisfied with his handiwork, he straightened up.

"What can I do for you today?" he asked.

Logan wasn't sure how much she should tell him—like everyone here, Jimmy had worked with the vet and seemed to have a good relationship with her. She knew the next words out of her mouth would bring the man pain, but she had to give him a reason for locking up the center and the police would be here soon. There just wasn't an easy way to say this.

"Louise asked me to tell you to close the center—lock every-thing up, close the gate, make sure no one comes in today," she said.

"O-kay . . ." Jimmy said, looking puzzled. "She say why?"

"There's been an accident . . ." Logan said.

"An accident? What kind of accident? Is anyone hurt? Is it Evka?" Jimmy asked, his voice rising with alarm.

Logan wondered why he assumed it was Evka. Probably because she usually arrived early.

"We're not sure what happened, Jimmy," Logan said, "but, yes, it was Evka. My friend and I found her this morning on the floor of one of the wards, but we don't know much more than that."

"When? How did she die?" he said. "It wasn't one of the raptors, was it? None of the animals would hurt her."

"I don't know. She was dead when we got there. It's not obvious what killed her, but it wasn't one of the raptors. It must have been last night or this morning. It had to be after I talked with her yesterday. She was fine then. The police and medical examiner will be able to figure all that out," Logan said. "They'll be here soon. You didn't happen to see anyone did you? Anyone come by after hours?"

"Um, we don't have security cameras. I got here just after seven, opened the gate about 7:30 a.m., usual time, then I've been back here. Didn't see anyone and wouldn't hear them with the saw going most the time, even if anyone was here," he said.

Swallowing hard, Jimmy took off his goggles and began peeling off his gloves. She wasn't sure, but it looked like the man was about to cry.

Logan felt awful.

"As soon as I know anything, I'll come find you and fill you in, I promise," Logan said. "In the meantime, when the police get here, bring them back to the hospital, okay? Louise is on her way in. If anyone else comes in this way, just send them home. Maybe put a sign out for visitors."

"Okay," he said. He quickly exited the shed and strode off in the direction of the front gate, removing the bunch of keys that hung from his belt loop by a carabiner.

Just then her phone rang. It was Louise.

"Be there in ten minutes, Logan," she said, "There's a key under the frog planter by the door, just outside my office. Let yourself in and wait for me. We'll divvy up meal prep and delivery, take care of any emergencies. If the police arrive before I do, I'll meet with them first in the animal hospital. I'll want to check on the two raptors, anyway. And if they need to talk with you first-you and your friend since you were the ones to discover the . . . her . . . then come find me as soon as you can."

Now that the original adrenaline was wearing off, Logan was very glad Louise was coming. Logan was a take charge person, but there was so much more to running the center and caring for the raptors than just the basic volunteer tasks she'd been taught to do. Today, she was very happy to be a foot soldier, not a general.

The rest of the morning went as smoothly as it could, given the circumstances. Louise reached Kit, the bird curator, who helped get the raptors' meals prepared and delivered while the police took Logan and Jean's initial statements.

The Lane County ME would be delayed by several hours, and Logan later learned that it wasn't unusual for one ME to ask another to help out. This apparently happened more often than one would think. Dead bodies don't care about issues like personnel cutbacks and budget shortfalls. They show up when they show up.

15

Jean was just finishing when the detectives arrived. They waited for her by the door. After introducing themselves as Detectives Voss and Tate and thanking her for stepping in, the short one, Voss, nodded toward the body.

"Well?"

"Given that she was clothed, but not heavily, and the temperature in the room is moderate, I can only tell you she died sometime between two and seven this morning," Jean said.

"No idea what killed her?" Tate asked.

"No. With no signs of a struggle, no wounds—defensive or otherwise—I'd only be guessing. You'll have to wait 'til they get her on the table," Jean said. "And probably won't know until after the autopsy."

"Yeah," Tate said.

"Bart's going to have 'em stacked up this weekend," Voss added. "It may take a while."

Jean nodded. If this was in Lincoln County, where she knew the detectives, she would have spoken more freely and suggested they try to move this body to the front of the line. Even without the office being trashed next door and the threat scrawled on the whiteboard, and given the woman's relatively young age and appearance of health, she would have easily called this a probable homicide, but it wasn't her call, it was theirs.

Still, she was curious. An unusual case. She'd have to give the ME a call later in the week and see what he could tell her. For now, she told them she was done, and they were free to take the body. Voss instructed one of the officers to send the EMTs back when the ambulance got there. They were probably already there, waiting in the parking lot. Since the center was closed, there was no problem taking her out the front.

The crime scene techs had taken pictures and would complete this room once the body was removed. They were almost done in the hallway and were now working on the hot mess in the office. None of the other rooms seemed to be disturbed, but she knew they'd go through all of them and eliminate prints, etc. The detectives kept Jean around a few more minutes, taking her preliminary statement.

They said they'd probably talk with her and Logan again, once they knew what they were dealing with, but for now they asked for her contact information and thanked her again for helping out. She gave Tate her card and said to tell the ME he could reach her at either of the two numbers listed there if he had any questions. One was for her medical practice in Lincoln City, the other her ME office in Newport. She was there most Wednesdays.

In addition, she gave them her cell number and the address of her rental house here in Eugene where she was staying tonight, then she left to go find Logan. Hopefully, Logan would be ready to leave soon. If not, Jean decided she would go get some work done at the house and come back to pick her up later.

This wasn't exactly the morning they had planned, but Jean was able to table her own personal feelings when she was doing her job. As medical examiner, examining dead bodies was fairly routine. If it *was* murder—and given the state of the office next door, she was pretty sure it was—she wondered how it went down. No obvious cause of death, no violence. Curious case.

After Jean left, Voss sent another uniform to take the handyman's statement and to send the director, a Louise Shimmel, back to be interviewed.

"We'll be in here," he said, pointing to ward 2, the room directly opposite Evka's office. They'd pulled in a couple of chairs from one of the other rooms.

*****

When Louise arrived a few minutes later—walking slowly, favoring her right knee—she couldn't help but see the wreckage and the threatening message scribbled on the white board. Her eyes narrowed, but she said nothing.

She saw the detectives waiting for her and walked in.

"How can I help you gentlemen?" she asked, taking the vacant chair opposite the two detectives. One was tall, bald, and very fit, dressed in a dark gray conservative suit. The other wore black slacks and jacket, a navy-blue polo shirt, with the name of the Eugene Police Department embroidered on it, and a ball cap. Both had what looked like guns under their jackets.

Holding their attention in her direct gaze, Louise straightened and stretched out her right leg a few times and rubbed her knee. She should have had the damn thing operated on last year, but things had just been too busy.

Notebook in hand, Tate, the tall, bald one, took lead. He had olive skin, Louise noted, which reminded her of the Argentinian family they'd lived next door to growing up. Their oldest boy, Pedro, had been her brother's best friend.

"Most of what we need right now is a list of all employees, volunteers, vendors, anyone who has access to the center and in particular, the animal hospital," Tate said. "Schedules, including deliveries. Particularly any time after midnight until the body was found this morning."

"No problem. I can get all that for you, but it's back in my office," she said.

Then she asked, "How did Evka die?"

Louise always took the direct approach.

"We're working on that," Tate said. "We're just getting our feet wet here. We'll escort you back to your office in a few minutes, but for now, anything you can tell us about Ms. . . . he looked at his notes . . . Novatna would be very helpful."

Voss jumped in. "Like, did she have any health issues? Heart trouble? Anything like that? Also, do you know of anyone who would have a reason to harm her?"

"No, she was in perfect health as far as I know," Louise said. "And to answer your second question, Evka was well-liked. Kept to herself, quiet, but everyone respected her."

"No problems with drugs or alcohol? Gambling?"

"No, of course not," Louise said, dismissing that possibility with a wave of her hand.

"How long had Ms. Novatna worked here?" asked Tate.

"I'd have to check my records for exact dates, but just over two years. It was about this time of year when I hired her, just before baby season," she said.

"Baby season?"

"Spring and summer. That's our busiest time of year, when all the raptors are breeding, we see a lot more birds then," she said. "Evka was a huge help."

Voss was also taking notes. Tate continued.

"What about her personal life? Domestic problems? Angry ex-husbands or boyfriends bothering her?" he asked. "Married male friends? Any jealous wives?"

He didn't glance at the trashed office across the hall, but he didn't have to. He knew Louise had seen it.

She looked him right in the eye.

"No, Evka wasn't married. As far as I know, she wasn't seeing anyone, but she's a private person, and I never asked her about her personal life. She did her job well."

Tate seemed to think about her response for a minute but decided for some reason not to continue down that road. Louise took advantage of the momentary lull.

"If we're almost done here, I really need to get back to the office," she said, standing, rubbing her knee before putting weight on it. "Someone needs to man the rescue line. If one of you wants to come with me, I'll be happy to get you Evka's employment records and a list of other staff and volunteers. Also, how long will we need to keep the center closed? I need to know what to tell everyone. I'll need to adjust some schedules."

"I can't give you anything exact," Tate said, "but I can promise you that everything that can be done is being done. By tomorrow we should be able to release the rest of the center for your staff to care for your birds here, but the hospital building and back entrance will be off limits until we're done."

"And how long will that be?"

"Until we're done."

16

Jean dropped Logan off at the house and went to pick up some basic groceries for the weekend. She had to be back to work on Monday, but Logan said she could stay the whole week as they had planned. Two more contractors were coming—one with a new window for the dining room and one to do the counters in the half bath. She promised Jean she'd be there to let them in and oversee the jobs. Death or not, life didn't stop.

After Jean left for the store, Logan pulled out one of the dining room chairs that looked out onto the side yard. She just needed a minute to sit.

Two hummingbird feeders hung from the eaves of the house next door. Only one had a visitor. She watched as the tiny bird fed greedily, but nervously, hovering above the feeder, dipping its beak into the yellow plastic flower opening again and again. When it landed briefly, it perched on the left edge of the ring, so she could only see it in profile.

She assumed it was a male Anna's hummingbird because of the bright, emerald-green back and the occasional flash of scarlet that flashed every time he jerked his head up to look around for predators, which was every few seconds. Ben always had throngs of these jeweled birds on his feeders back in Jasper year-round, but here, there was just the one.

As Logan watched, the only danger that came this Anna's way was another hummingbird, who kept dive bombing him, driving him away just long enough to zoom in and steal a drink. Then the first one would come back and regain his position. Rinse and repeat. It was ridiculous. There were seven holes around the feeder, and it was full of sugar water. Plenty for all. Why didn't they just share?

The thought made her wonder if humans and hummingbirds were the only two species whose main threats came from members of our own kind.

She got up to make a pot of coffee. It was already past noon, but she figured she'd be so tired tonight, the extra caffeine wouldn't keep her awake. Besides, she needed something warm and comforting right now.

This morning she'd been too busy helping Louise with the animals then giving her statement to the police to really think about Evka's death. But now, in the silent house, it all came flooding back.

She smelled the burnt coffee as she and Jean walked down the hall, saw the destruction they found in the office, and then Evka—sprawled on the floor. And of course, the dead hawk behind the door. His neck had been bent at an odd angle. Did that happen when he flew into the wall or did someone break it? Had someone killed them both? And if so, why. . . and in Evka's case, how?

An incoming call on her cell phone interrupted Logan's thoughts. She went back inside and looked at the caller. It was Sam.

Damn. She'd forgotten Sam was coming. She tapped the screen to take the call.

"Hi, Sam," she said.

IN PLAIN SIGHT

As usual, she had to wait for her friend to take a breath before she could break into the conversation.

". . . I'm about twenty minutes out," Sam babbled. "What are you guys in the mood for? I'm thinking pizza. Hope a late lunch is okay—have you already eaten? Sorry I couldn't get on the road earlier. I'll get two large pizzas and we'll have leftovers . . . maybe. Meat lovers and whatever you two want. I assume Jean wants to add veggies. Anything else you want me to pick up?"

Finally, Logan got a word in, "No, thanks, Sam. Jean's at the store. I'm sure she'll get whatever else we need. And yeah, make the second pizza half veggies and half whatever else sounds good."

"You don't sound good," Sam said. "Is something wrong?"

No hiding anything from Sam. Her nose for news translated into her personal life, too.

"No, I'm fine. We had kind of a bad morning," *understatement of the century*, she thought, "but don't worry. We're okay. I'll fill you in when you get here," Logan said, disconnecting the call before Sam could ask any more questions.

As a professional journalist, Sam was perfectly capable of handling bad news while driving—in fact, she thrived on it. She'd worked the crime beat in Olympia, Washington before moving to the small, coastal town of Newport for love. But Logan just couldn't bring herself to talk about it over the phone. She was surprised at how much this was affecting her.

It's not that she'd never seen a dead body. She had. Just last year a dog she was walking for a friend dragged her over to where a woman had been shot just minutes before—but she didn't know that woman well. And what she'd heard of her hadn't been very complimentary.

Evka was different. Logan had worked in close quarters with the kind woman for months, learning from her, laughing with her, staying up all night to nurse the injured hawk. And

Wednesday, after Mia barged in and then stormed out, she and Evka shared confessions and personal life stories until the wee hours. Logan even found herself opening up to her about Jack and her discovery of his cheating just after he died.

Then, as the moon pulled a velvet blanket over itself and made way for the stars, she told Evka about her mother's abandonment of her and her brother, Rick, when she was thirteen and he was nine. And then about their mother's return to their lives, bringing along a half-sister she never knew she had. Logan rarely shared such intimate details of her own life with anyone, but it just felt right. And the bourbon hadn't hurt.

17

Logan and Jean were just finishing putting the groceries away—yogurt, paleo granola, lots of leafy greens, skinless chicken breasts, pasture-raised eggs and butter, more coffee, a few bottles of wine—everything organic and non-GMO—when Sam arrived. Logan knew Sam would make another run to the store later to stock up on her own essential items: Double Stuf Oreos, diet soda, and the makings for killer nachos. At least they all would agree on the wine. Anything Jean selected would be great.

Sam deposited the pizza boxes on the table, dumped out the bag of napkins and little packets, and plopped down. Adding hot pepper flakes to a steaming slice of the meat lovers, she took a huge bite.

Still chewing, she wiped her mouth with one of the takeout napkins and pointed to the empty chairs.

"Sit! Spill!" she said. "Tell me everything."

Logan and Jean did as she commanded and between bites filled her in on the morning's events. Sam went into reporter mode, but Logan had almost as many questions since she hadn't been there for Jean's examination of the body.

"So no idea how she died?" Sam asked.

"If it wasn't for the violence done in her office and the threatening message on the whiteboard, I would say it looked like a heart attack or some other natural cause," Jean said. "There were no signs of a struggle or any indication she had been attacked."

"What will they do with the hawk?" Sam asked.

Logan answered that one, "The center will probably do a necropsy on it. I think the law requires an animal autopsy be done on any raptor they lose under unknown circumstances."

The visual image of the dead bird they had taken such great pains to heal was one she wished she could stop seeing. The numbness was starting to wear off, with anger taking its place.

"I just wish I knew what happened in that building," Logan said. "Evka was such a good person. I can't believe she's dead. Not that good people can't die, of course. I mean, did someone trash her office then kill her? If she was killed, how? And if she was there in ward 3, why didn't she go in and confront whoever it was—there's no way she wouldn't have heard them in there throwing things around. Those walls are paper thin."

For a few minutes, the three women were silent.

Then Jean said, "I left a message for Bart."

"Bart who?" Logan asked.

"Bart Nelson, the Lane County ME," she said. "He's the one I stood in for this morning. He was out on a multiple car pileup, that's why they asked me to help. He called me back. Said he can put off the auto accident victims, since the cause of death is known, but he still has a possible suicide to do. Evka's autopsy probably won't happen until Monday, but he'll let me know what he finds."

"That's great!" Logan said. "Is he allowed to do that?"

"Not officially, but I met Bart at a conference last year and he doesn't mind sharing—unofficially."

Jean batted her eyelashes and gave a Cheshire grin.

"And I'm already here for the weekend . . ." Sam said, catching on. "I'm not without *some* skills . . ."

Some skills was putting it mildly. Sam had been an award-winning investigative reporter in the big city until she moved to the coast for love. Logan wanted to hug her.

"So what are we waiting for?" Sam said. "Let's get rid of these pizza boxes. You have WIFI here yet, Jean?"

"Indeed, I do," Jean said.

Sam punched her fist in the air. "The Cormorant Coffee Crew rides again!"

This time, Logan hugged her friends for real.

For the next hour, the three women made a plan and divvied up first tasks. As the one with the most investigative experience, Sam took the lead.

"Until we hear from Jean's friend on Monday, the most productive thing we can do is get the best picture of Evka's life that we can. That's what the cops will do. Plus follow up on any leads they uncover at the scene."

"I assume they'll investigate this like a murder even if they don't know for sure. Right?" Logan asked.

"If they're any good, they will," Sam said. "Better to treat it like a homicide and gather information and evidence before it gets lost. I'll check with my contacts in Newport. Somebody might know somebody out here."

"But we are not without resources," she added, retrieving her computer from her bag. "We need to build a picture of Evka's life. Logan, since you worked with her, what do you know about her? Family, friends, anything."

Logan was hesitant to share Evka's secrets, but realized it was silly to worry about that now. She briefly summarized what she knew and told them about Mia's short, but memorable appearance at Evka's home.

"What's Mia's last name? And who else knows about her and Evka?" Sam asked.

"I don't know," Logan said. "No one else would, either, at least not at the center. Evka was pretty clear she was keeping all of that private. But someone could have found out."

"If they did, the police will find out and they'll certainly want to talk with this Mia," Jean said. "Do you think she did it?"

"I don't know," Logan said. "I can see her as being angry enough—she was furious with Evka that night, and she's perfectly capable of trashing an office—but wouldn't her message say something else? It said, 'Back off, Bitch!' If Mia wrote that, what did it mean? She wanted Evka to come closer, to be truthful about their relationship, to come out in the open, not to back away from something or someone."

Sam made a note of that. She already had several files going on her own laptop. Two Excel spreadsheets, one with a time-line of events and one with Evka's basic bio and the names of everyone she knew. There was no family alive that Logan knew about, but she could ask Louise.

"Do you know how to get in touch with her?" Sam asked.

"Mia? No," I don't even know where she's staying," Logan said. "No, wait! I forgot—Evka said she works down in Newport at the Hatfield Marine Science Center. They'd have her contact information."

"Yes, but they're not going to give it to us," Sam said. "We need to get down there. We should talk with her before the police do. At least see if she's still in the area."

Jean volunteered since she was going back Monday anyway. No one knew what Mia's hours were—if she worked weekends or not.

"We may need to go before then. The cops will probably find out about Mia through Evka's phone. There will be a record of calls and texts between them. Did either of you see her phone at the scene?"

Logan and Jean looked at each other. "No, I didn't see one, but it must be there somewhere. Maybe in her office?" Logan said. "No one goes anywhere without their phone."

Sam added that to the list of things they needed to find out, and Jean said she'd ask Bart if it was on her person when he got her. In a pocket, maybe."

She also said she could go back early and drive over to Hatfield Marine Science Center and see if she could track Mia down over the weekend. They looked online and it was open from ten to four both Saturday and Sunday.

"Okay," Sam said. "Moving on to coworkers."

Logan could answer this question in a fair amount of detail.

She gave Sam a list of the people Evka usually worked with on a daily basis, including volunteers: Neil, Aaron, Jimmy, Chrissie and a couple of other volunteers, the man who delivered the live chicks, and, of course, Louise, the director. Once they exhausted these options, she would figure out a way to try to get the whole list.

It was unlikely Louise would let her just wander through the personnel files, which would probably violate nine different privacy laws. Hopefully, before she had to ask, the police would have solved the case, but she wasn't holding her breath.

Later that night, as she lay on a very comfortable queen-sized bed in one of Jean's newly refurbished guest bedrooms, Logan found herself staring at the ceiling, unable to sleep.

Why was there so much evil in the world? Who would want to murder this gentle woman—a highly skilled veterinarian who spent her life easing the suffering of animals, helping them enjoy the fullest and longest lives possible after hopefully being returned to the wild? Whoever had killed Evka had caused the death of the red-tail hawk, too, even if inadvertently.

Determination settled in Logan's heart. These deaths would not go unanswered.

18

"**S**hit," Tate swore and tossed the phone back onto his desk. *Damn these new phones.*

Voss looked up. "What?"

"Fingerprint protected," Tate grumbled, staring at the offending piece of technology.

"Can't we get Bart to help out? I mean . . . our girl still has fingers, right?" Voss said.

"That only works in the movies," Tate said, closing his eyes to concentrate.

Actually, a post-mortem fingertip press—grisly as that picture was to consider—might have worked if he'd done it at the scene while the body was still fresh, but he hadn't wanted to break into the dead woman's phone in front of the Lincoln County ME. Technically, it was legal to get into it—a dead person had no expected rights to privacy, but it was a fuzzy enough area and he didn't know how much of a stickler the visiting ME was. From her brisk efficiency at the scene, she looked like the type who went by the rules.

It was a moot point now anyway. He knew that once a body lost its conductivity and warmth, it could no longer trigger a fingerprint sensor. He wasn't even sure the phone was hers. It had been found under a pile of papers and an in-basket that had been swept off the vet's desk onto the floor in her office. Whomever it belonged to, they'd need a warrant to get the phone records. He had Voss add that to the growing list.

This would slow them down, but for now, they still had plenty to do. Bart was loaded up with a possible suicide along with the multiple pileup victims. Even working the weekend, he wouldn't have autopsy results until Monday.

After they grabbed some lunch, Tate and Voss would spend the rest of the day canvassing the neighborhood surrounding the center to see if anyone saw or heard anything. It's a shame it was a residential area. There wouldn't be any CTV coverage unless someone had a home security camera facing the street. Maybe they'd get lucky. You never knew.

This weekend would consist of going over statements and interviewing anyone and everyone they couldn't reach today—getting to know their victim—assuming it was murder—which it almost certainly was. They'd also get the prints run through AFIS and take a look at whatever else the crime scene techs dug up. Time was critical, so they had to go on that assumption unless the autopsy proved otherwise.

Tate checked his messages first, but nothing more urgent than their current case had come in this morning. Eugene wasn't a big murder town. They only averaged about five homicides a year. Even though he felt bad for the woman who died, Tate couldn't help but also feel a small rise of excitement he'd never admit to.

"*Cornucopia Kitchen,* okay?" Tate asked as he scooped up his keys.

"Think they can do their chicken pot pie to go?" Voss asked.

Tate pictured the large, messy pie.

"We'll eat there, but make it quick," Tate said. It was that or let the man eat in the car. Even though it belonged to the department, he felt obligated to clean it. And any car Voss ate in needed to be cleaned.

*****

When they arrived at the center, they each took opposite sides of the street and started knocking on doors. About half of the homes had someone home. Only one had a camera and it had been knocked sideways and only produced a record of their own cars and a trail of very industrious ants on their driveway. They crossed off the ones whose owners they'd been able to talk with and noted the remaining houses. They'd try again tonight after rush hour, when hopefully, commuters would return home and they'd have better luck.

In the meantime, they decided to talk to the handyman if he was still around.

"Vogel took his statement, but it's pretty sparse," Voss said as Tate drove.

"Yeah," Tate agreed. Vogel wasn't the sharpest tool in the shed.

They started to park outside the barrier, but Jimmy saw them and ambled over to let them in. He'd been working on a wooden railing on the side of a ramp that led up to the gift shop. The detectives introduced themselves and asked if there was some place they could talk. Jimmy said Louise was in her office, but they could use his workshop.

Pulling out two folding camp chairs for his guests, Jimmy said, "Sorry, I don't have anything more comfortable."

Tate said they were fine. Jimmy half sat on the edge of a worktable he had in the middle of the room and wiped his hands on a rag he pulled from the pocket of his jeans. "What can I do for you?" he said. "How can I help?"

Tate noticed the man's eyes were slightly bloodshot. Could be from the sawdust, or the fact that one of his coworkers had just died. He wondered how close Jimmy and the vet had been.

Tate began with the routine questions Vogel had already gone over, then asked Jimmy who the vet had been friends with at the center, or if he knew if she was involved with anyone—did she have a boyfriend or had she had one who might be upset enough to trash her office and kill her?

"Everyone liked Evka, but she wasn't close to anyone here— in that way," he said. "And if she had a boyfriend, she never said."

"She never went out after work with any of the staff?" Tate asked. "Out to dinner?"

"No," Jimmy said, "Not that I know of. She joined us if Louise took everyone out, which she did on occasion."

Tate waited.

Jimmy filled in the blank.

"Well, I mean, she was friendly, but really, only the younger staff and the volunteers socialize after work. I think they sometimes meet up for pizza or beer. Some of the volunteers know each other from the college, but other than our annual Christmas party, which we hold in the office area, the staff here just works, then goes home at the end of the day. We're all pretty bushed."

"Anyone stay late or come in early?" Tate asked.

"Sure, when they need to. The raptors don't keep a nine to five schedule. Louise and Evka work the longest hours, and sometimes Neil or Aaron if there's more than one rescue pickup. Evka sometimes needs an extra hand during the busy season. Everyone pitches in."

"Okay. Thank you. Now, I know you went over all this before, but before we leave, if you could go over your exact movements this morning, from your time of arrival to when you opened the gate for Ms. McKenna and Mrs. Pullman, that would be very helpful."

Tate nodded as Jimmy went through his usual routines. Each morning, he arrived between 7:00 and 7:30 a.m., worked on whatever needed doing. Some mornings he'd go back and have a cup of coffee with Evka if she was in, but today he was working on the railing, so he hadn't gone back to the animal hospital at all. At 8:00 a.m., he opened the gate.

Tate listened and jotted a few more notes, then asked Jimmy to verify all of the points of ingress and egress that Louise had already identified for them when they'd walked the center with her earlier in the day, just in case they missed any.

When they finished up, Tate thanked Jimmy for his time and gave him his card. "If you remember anything or need to get in touch with us, you can reach us at these numbers anytime."

Jimmy took the card and watched as the two detectives walked back to their car.

19

"**Y**ou just sit right here and get comfortable, Aaron," Chrissie said, guiding her patient into the living room and lowering him onto the couch. "The remote is on the table. You find something to watch while I get you an ice pack. I'll be right back."

Oh, God . . . Nurse Chrissie . . . that's all I need. Should have Ubered it.

Loud, banging noises emitted from the kitchen.

Chrissie returned with a glass of water and a makeshift ice pack consisting of smashed ice cubes in a baggie, wrapped in a dish towel. After handing it to him, she put her hands on her hips and surveyed the scene.

"Looks like you don't have a throw or anything. Do you have any extra blankets? If not, I'll just grab some off your bed," she said.

Pressing the ice pack against the left side of his face, Aaron pointed toward the hallway.

The dentist had given him prescriptions for Vicodin and hydrocodone, which Chrissie said she'd pick up later. The anesthetic was still numbing everything, but they'd told him he'd be needing something soon.

As much as he didn't want Chrissie there, he did appreciate the ride, the ice pack, and the prescriptions pickup. He just hoped she'd leave after that. All he wanted to do was zone out and hopefully fall asleep watching Bourne Identity for the eighteenth time. Alone.

He bit down harder on the gauze pack and hoped she'd find the hall closet. The last thing he wanted was for Chrissie to go into his bedroom.

She returned with a pillow and a wool blanket, which she tucked around her reluctant patient.

"Now, you sit tight, and I'll be right back!" she said. "Don't you worry, Aaron, I'll take care of you."

When he heard the front door click shut, he let out a breath and closed his eyes. It was no big deal. Chrissie just had a crush on him. After this, he would avoid her. He knew how to handle these kids. And Chrissie was just that. A kid. What was she, twenty-something? Probably barely legal to buy alcohol. Just out of college, gung-ho to save the planet, with no idea how to do it. Maybe he could set her up with one of the other volunteers. Van was about her age. Yeah, that would do it. He'd set them up when he got back next week.

He took a deep breath and settled back into the couch but didn't turn on the TV. He'd watch his movie after she left. Instead, he allowed his mind to wander on the last waves of anesthesia. Images of Evka filled his mind.

Evka, leaning over one of her charges, her long, slender fingers tenderly cleaning a wound or laughing when a baby barn owl stretched its neck out to greedily grab a morsel of meat she offered him from a pair of tweezers. And then, that night . . . oh . . . he'd never forget that night.

IN PLAIN SIGHT

He got hot just thinking about it.

It all had started two years ago. Louise told them they were getting a new vet, one from Africa, who'd been running a big game animal hospital in Kenya. He remembered exactly where he was standing when she came in. He was in ward 2, recording the weight of one of their new patients, a young, female turkey vulture. Marker in hand, he looked up and for a moment, he was floored.

It wasn't that Evka was pretty in the traditional sense, but a true beauty flowed from her features. Dark, glossy hair, kind eyes, firm body. And when she moved . . . effortless, graceful. When Louise introduced her to everyone, he'd managed to keep his cool, but he didn't get up to shake her hand. If he had, they would have seen his erection.

For the next few months, they worked side by side. The vet assistant left with the previous vet. He was filling in until they found another one. It was the busy season, and they pulled several all-nighters. He had no serious girlfriend at the time, and as far as he could tell, Evka wasn't seeing anyone. They settled into a comfortable routine.

Both were serious advocates for wildlife. He only had his masters but was considering going for his PhD. He wanted to be Evka's equal. He started envisioning them starting a wildlife hospital somewhere together. Borneo, maybe. They were good together, he knew, but he was careful not to share his feelings, yet. He didn't want to screw this up. Something about Evka was different. He bided his time.

One night, around eleven, Evka's cell rang. When she glanced at the screen, her expression immediately darkened, and she stalked back to her office to take the call. A few minutes later, she returned, obviously upset. He'd asked her if she was okay. She'd looked up and said, in her soft, Czech accent, 'No. No, Aaron, I am *not* okay!'

What happened next was the happiest surprise of his life. She looked right at him and asked if he wanted to go get a drink with her. He immediately agreed.

It was just supposed to be a short stop on the way home, but one drink turned into two and then he was offering her a ride—she was in no condition to drive, but then, neither was he. It's a wonder they made it to her place in one piece.

Safe inside, they made it only as far as the couch. It all felt so urgent and raw, like they were the first two people who's ever made love. She climbed on top. Then, he was undoing her thick braid, letting her hair fall all around him, breathing in the scent of her, wanting nothing more than to make her the happiest woman on the planet. And by the sounds she let loose from deep in her throat as she arched her back, she was.

But that was it.

The next morning, she was up before he was, fully dressed, sitting at the kitchen table with a mug of coffee. She said nothing, just handed him a piping hot to-go cup waiting on the counter. Very thoughtful.

That was over year ago and they hadn't spoken about it since. But that didn't mean he didn't think about it.

"Yoo-hoo!" Chrissie called as she let herself in the front door. "I'm b-a-ck and I've got your drugs!"

20

Aaron sat up straighter on the couch, listening to Chrissie making herself at home. She'd breezed right in, announced her arrival, and gone straight back to the kitchen. He could hear her putting away the groceries she had picked up along with his prescriptions. He hadn't asked her to do that. He'd have to pay her, at least, but maybe later—the thought of moving was more than he could manage right this second. He just wanted her to go home.

Next, he heard her opening the freezer, scooping ice cubes into something, then running some water, then bang around in the cupboards and silverware drawer. What was she doing in there?

When she returned, she had a fresh makeshift ice pack and another glass of water. She replaced the ice pack and adjusted the towel against his jaw.

He tried to talk around the gauze in his mouth, to get out a thank you, tell her he was fine now and could manage on his own, she could *leave*, but she didn't take the hint. Instead, she went back into the kitchen to retrieve the small white paper bag that held his prescriptions and a bowl of ice cream with a spoon. She put the bowl on the coffee table and pulled out one of the prescriptions—he hoped it was for pain meds—and started reading the label.

"Let's see now," she said, squinting, "It says here to take one of these as needed, but no more than one every four hours, and you need to take it with food. Now, they said only *soft* foods, so I picked up some yogurt and ice cream, stuff like that. I didn't know if you liked chocolate or vanilla, so I got both. I'm giving you the ice cream first because they said the cold might help."

Next, she started to hand him the bowl—the ice cream did look really good—but when it looked like she was going to try to spoon feed him, he pushed the bowl away.

"Nnno hank you, rissie," he said, hoping she could under-stand him as he talked around the gauze. "You khan lev, I khan do ih mysef."

She looked puzzled and tried again. Aaron again pushed the bowl away, this time a little more firmly. He may not have been able to speak clearly, but the look in his eyes was clear enough. Chrissie got the message.

She put the bowl down and carefully sat next to him on the couch, a look of deep concern in her eyes. "I'm so sorry, honey," she said. "I should have asked you what you wanted. Do you want something else to eat? You don't have to have the ice cream. I can get you some yogurt if you want. Or I got some instant mashed potatoes I can make . . ."

Aaron squeezed his eyes shut.

This chick is so dense. How can anyone be so stupid?

Then, she reached out and put her hand on his thigh, squeezing it, then patted his knee, "Don't worry, just tell me what you need. I'm here for you. That's what girlfriends do!"

IN PLAIN SIGHT

This time, Aaron pushed her hand away—and none too gently.

"You are NOH my girfrien'!" he tried to say, glaring at her.

He wanted to say more, that he appreciated the ride, the drugs, and even the ice cream, but he'd knocked something loose in his mouth. He needed to clamp down hard on the gauze roll they'd given him to stop the bleeding. He'd have to explain it all to her later. Right now, he just needed her to leave! He couldn't let her keep thinking his allowing her to help him meant anything more than taking up a friend on their offer. He should have known this wasn't a good idea, but Neil was out of town and everyone else was busy.

For a minute, Chrissie sat stunned, as if what he said didn't make sense. When she finally absorbed the verbal blow, her transformation from fawning nursemaid to furious woman was almost instantaneous. She jumped onto her feet, fists clenched by her sides, and towered over him.

"Well, Evka's not your girlfriend, either, is she?" she said. "Your precious Evka couldn't be bothered to help you, could she? I was here for you, not her!"

Aaron's eyes grew wide.

"You didn't think I knew, did you?" she said, stomping around the coffee table. "Well, everybody knows, Aaron! You've been mooning over her from the minute she got here. But she won't give you the time of day, will she?"

"No, you can't see what's right in front of your face! ME!"

With this, Chrissie jerked up her t-shirt and showed him her breasts. "You could have had *these*, buddy boy. I'll bet Evka's boobs aren't nearly as perky. In fact, she hardly has any! Old crone! What is she, twenty years older than you? You're sick!"

Shaking with fury, Chrissie looked like she wanted to punch him in the face. Aaron pushed back into the couch cushions as far as he could, but instead of taking out her anger directly on him, she grabbed the bowl of ice cream and threw it across the room. Then, she opened up his bottle of pain pills and shook them out all over the floor.

"There!" she said.

Aaron remained very still. It looked like she was winding up to yell some more, but she must not have been able to think of insults strong enough, because all she did was work her jaw back and forth, looking extremely frustrated.

Finally, Chrissie burst into tears, grabbed her car keys and coat, and stormed out, slamming the door behind her so hard a picture in the bedroom crashed onto the floor.

"You're going to wish you made a better *choice*, Aaron!"

21

THURSDAY, FEBRUARY 24

Chrissie threw her truck into reverse and screeched out of Aaron's driveway. Straight armed, clenching the steering wheel at ten and two, she gunned the engine and raced down the residential street. The burst of speed felt satisfying, but she wasn't completely stupid. She didn't need another ticket. She had just turned twenty-one, but her dad held the title to the truck. Another ticket and her wheels were history.

By the time she got to the light, she'd gotten her emotions somewhat under control. A leftover burst of anger spiked, and she banged the heel of her hand on the dashboard.

That bastard!

How was she ever going to work with him again? She'd be so embarrassed! She wished she'd never set eyes on Aaron Whitlock. What a dweeb! She'd just wasted a year of her life mooning over a guy who had no interest in her.

When she got to the turn off for her street, she looked at the clock. 5:30 p.m.

Damn.

This was about the time all the moms came to pick up their kids. Her mom ran a licensed daycare center out of the house. Her dad had converted the large family room into a playroom. Without a college degree, her mom made more money watching other people's kids than going out to work herself.

Chrissie used to help her out when it was just babysitting and when her mom got a daycare license, she'd hired Chrissie officially for ten to fifteen hours a week. It was a good gig. The hours were flexible, and she could fit it around her course schedule at the community college.

Chrissie knew all the moms and normally enjoyed stopping to chat when they picked up their kids, but not today. Today, talking was the last thing she felt like doing. So instead of turning right, she continued on straight. The car practically drove itself to Lone Star.

It was a little early to start drinking, but she'd skipped lunch. She hadn't wanted to miss the phone call from the dental office. They said they'd call when Aaron was ready to go.

Anger again surged through her at doing favors for someone who didn't appreciate them.

There were only a few patrons in the place. Chrissie ordered a burger and fries at the bar and a beer, then chose a dark booth in the back to eat, drink, and nurse her wounds. At seven o'clock, she figured it was safe to go home. On the way, she stopped at a liquor store and bought a bottle of vodka and some cranberry juice. Another advantage of living on her own—her parents were pretty good about respecting her privacy. They wanted her to become an adult. Well, if getting your heart broken was what it took to become an adult, she'd have her graduation ceremony tonight.

For the next couple of hours, Chrissie made herself several ersatz cosmos. She didn't have lime juice or whatever else it was they put in those, nor did she have one of those metal martini shakers or a fancy martini glass, so they weren't all pretty and icy like they were when she and her friends ordered them at the club, but with some ice cubes in a water glass, they tasted okay.

As the evening progressed, anger with Aaron began to morph into anger at Evka. She was the Evil Older Woman Temptress, not the mild-mannered, nice veterinarian everyone thought she was. No, it wasn't Aaron's fault.

If Evka hadn't come between them, she and Aaron would be together by now. They were the right age; they had the same interests. They looked good together. Hell, they'd probably be engaged and planning their wedding. But, nooo! Greedy Evka got her claws in him! Someone needed to set her straight.

Around midnight, Chrissie had polished off most of the bottle. She attempted to screw the cap back on but missed. She scowled at the bottle, then gave up. Vodka didn't go bad. She'd clean this up in the morning. Her dad never came in here, but she knew her mom sometimes checked up on her. She didn't need another lecture.

Bleary eyed, she stood up from the kitchen table and made her way across the floor toward her bed. The room started spinning. She breathed carefully and closed her eyes, willing it to stop.

It didn't.

Using the walls to steady herself, she hurried toward the bathroom. When she got there, she sank to her knees in front of the toilet. Then she proceeded to puke her guts out in wave after wave of pink vomit. At some point, she fell asleep on the bathroom floor, curled up on the pink bathmat her mother had given her when she moved in. She'd called it her "garage warming present." Her mom thought she was funny.

Around three in the morning, Chrissie woke up freezing and pried one eye open. Freezing and stiff, she carefully got up and rinsed her mouth out with cold water. She felt like death and one look in the mirror confirmed it. She'd have to call in sick tomorrow . . . today.

Turning on the shower, Chrissie made a decision. This was all Evka's fault. Evka wasn't going to leave Aaron alone until someone spelled it out for her and Aaron certainly wasn't going to do it. He was still under her spell. It was up to her.

Dropping last night's clothes into the hamper, she showered in record time. Next, she pulled on a fresh pair of jeans and sweatshirt, then ran a brush through her hair and swiped on some mascara and lip gloss. She wished she had time to make herself look better, but she wanted to get this over with before she lost her nerve.

Grabbing her keys and pulling on her boots, she quietly let herself out the door. Her parents slept like logs, but she put the truck in neutral and let it roll down the driveway to the street. Before starting it up, she consulted her phone. She didn't know Evka's exact address, she'd only been there once. The vet had hosted a staff get together at her house a few months ago. She started scrolling through the locations. Score! Google maps found it right away. Good thing her phone had a better memory than she did.

Before she lost her nerve, Chrissie tapped in a quick text. Satisfied with what she wrote, she hit send, then propped her phone in one of the cup holders. Next, she started up her truck and turned 'right at the light' as instructed. She felt stone cold sober and ready to tackle this problem head on. Woman to woman!

The direct approach was always best. This shouldn't take long. She'd tell her to leave Aaron alone and make sure she understood she meant it.

By the time the first daycare kids arrived at her mom's house, she'd be tucked into bed, getting some much-deserved sleep. She was off Fridays and didn't have a class until two o'clock.

22

MONDAY MORNING, FEBRUARY 28

CASCADES RAPTOR CENTER

Gripping the railing to take the pressure off her knee, Louise walked up the ramp that led to her office and the gift shop area. Behind her, Jimmy gave the front gate a final tug, making sure it would stay open for staff as they arrived for the special staff meeting Louise had called, then followed her in.

"Nice job, Jimmy," Louise said.

Jimmy nodded.

A throw-back from the seventies, the admin building was octagonal, with several offices and storage rooms surrounding an open, center area with long, dark, wooden beams meeting at a point overhead. A short hallway led to the gift shop, which had an exterior door for the public.

"Do you want more chairs, or is this enough?" Jimmy asked.

A couple dozen folding, metal chairs had been arranged in a semi-circle, facing a chair next to a small table for Louise.

"No, this should do," she said. "I'm not sure how many of the volunteers will make it in. Some of them have classes today."

"I can always bring in more if you need them," he said.

"Sounds good," she said. "Why don't you get yourself some coffee, Jimmy. I'm going to keep the phones set to the recording. Remind me to switch it back when we're done."

She'd set the meeting for 8:30 a.m. There really was no rush, they weren't opening the center today. For one thing, the animal hospital was still cordoned off with crime scene tape. For another, she didn't anticipate anyone would feel like working after she delivered the news. A few people knew already, of course, but to most of the staff, Evka's death would come as a shock.

The police had been here all weekend. Even though the animal hospital was off limits, Louise had insisted on caring for the two remaining avian patients, so they allowed her—under supervision—to move the two injured raptors to ward 1, which was farthest away from Evka's office and ward 3 where she was found. They also allowed her to remove the dead red-tail hawk, but not until he had been photographed from every angle, samples taken, and any fibers or whatever they were looking for, had been collected from his body. She asked if they found anything significant, but nobody was telling her anything.

Staff members and volunteers started trickling in, and by 8:30 a.m. it looked like most everyone was here. Aaron, his jaw still swollen from his surgery last week, sat in the back, looking miserable. Logan McKenna sat on the side, where she could see everyone. Since she got here early, Louise had given Logan the task of checking everyone's name off the staff list as they filtered in. Kit, Chrissie, Julie, Neil—oh good, Neil was back—Ulrike, Carrie, Brian, Danny . . .

"Good morning, everyone, grab some coffee and get some food—there are donuts and granola bars in the back. I think Carrie brought some fruit. Then I'd like to get started," Louise said. Most had already done so and the few remaining staff in the back came and found a seat.

"Those of you who had Friday shifts already know that we closed the center, and it will be closed again today. Hopefully, we will be able to open tomorrow. So keep your phones charged. I'll let you know tonight. After this meeting, I'll have a few core staff stay and see to the essentials, but everyone else will return home until you receive a call from me," she said.

Next, she turned to Tim, one of the volunteers who helped out in the animal hospital. "Tim, I know the police have already contacted you. I appreciate you not sharing that information with anyone until I had a chance to speak with everyone this morning and call those who could not attend this meeting."

Puzzled looks and murmurs.

Louise then addressed the whole group, "I promise I'll answer all of the questions that I can, just let me get through this part first . . . Most of you knew, or at least have met our veterinarian, Evka Novatna. There's no easy way to say this. Friday morning, Evka was found dead in the animal hospital."

"Oh my God!"

"What?"

"How?"

"Was there an accident?"

"Was she sick?"

Louise held her hands, palms out, to quiet the group, "We don't know. There was no sign of an accident and the raptor she was treating unfortunately died also."

"How?"

"What happened?"

"They were both found in ward 3. The raptor was out of his kennel," Louise said. "Evka was found on the floor—no signs of violence—and the red-tail was discovered behind the door."

Logan noted that she did not mention the violence done to Evka's office. Maybe the police were holding back that piece of information in the hopes of catching someone who might slip and mention it.

As Louise fielded questions, Logan took the opportunity to observe the reactions of those she knew had worked closest with Evka.

Aaron's face drained of all color. She thought he was going to pass out, but he gripped his chair and remained upright. Jimmy already knew, of course. He remained taciturn, leaning against the back wall by the coffee and donuts, arms folded, his baseball cap pulled low. He'd had several days to process Evka's death.

Chrissie looked shell-shocked. She sat wide-eyed and stunned, her mouth slightly agape. Neil, who was back from his vacation, looked straight ahead, then took a sip of his coffee. Stoic. She supposed Neil was of that generation of men taught not to show their emotions. Kit and Carrie clasped hands. Carrie started crying. Kit put her arm around the woman, a few tears leaking out of her own eyes, too.

Watching the varied reactions, Logan felt a shiver up her spine. Could one of these people have killed Evka? Were any of them capable of murder?

After she had answered all of the questions she could or was going to, Louise summed up the situation, "Although there were no signs of physical attack, because the cause of her death is still undetermined, the police are conducting a thorough investigation."

She didn't say homicide, but everyone got the idea. She hurried on before anyone could ask another question.

"So," she continued briskly, "the animal hospital is still off limits, but hopefully, it will be released soon. The police will be talking with those of us who worked with Evka, so don't be alarmed when and if the police contact you to ask a few questions. Jimmy, Logan, and I gave statements Friday, and it didn't take long. Just answer as best you can. If you don't know something, just say so or refer them to me. If anyone here knows anything that might be helpful, you can talk to me or call them before they call you."

She walked over to the whiteboard and wrote Detective Tate's name and phone number on it. "This is the detective in charge."

"For today, we'll just take care of the absolutely essential needs of the raptors. Kit, why don't you and Aaron take care of the residents, I'll check on the two injured we have left. They're allowing us access to ward 1 on the far end of the animal hospital, the farthest away from where Evka was found."

Next, she turned to Chrissie, who had called in sick on Friday.

"Chrissie, you were scheduled for this morning—since you're here I assume you're feeling better?"

Chrissie nodded.

"Good . . . and Logan, if you could stay and help Chrissie, that'd be great. I have work in the office, but Aaron and Kit will join you as soon as they finish their rounds."

"Okay, that should do it. Everyone else, thank you for coming in. Hopefully, we'll be back to our regular schedule tomorrow, so don't change your calendars yet. Either way, I will let you know by tonight."

People milled and talked, but when it was obvious Jimmy was waiting for them to leave so he could lock the gate, they allowed themselves to be herded out the door toward their cars.

Logan was very grateful Louise had not mentioned that she was the one who discovered Evka's body. She didn't want to relive that memory and she sure as hell didn't want to answer anyone's ghoulish questions about it.

23

Thursday, after Chrissie peeled out of his driveway, Aaron managed to find all but one of the Vicodin and all of the hydrocodone tablets she'd dumped out on the floor. He then cleaned up the melted ice cream mess as best he could. Finally, he got himself a fresh bowl of vanilla ice cream, popped two pills and put himself to bed, where he'd stayed for the remainder of the weekend.

Sunday night he resurrected long enough to take a shower and polish off the last of the yogurt. Although his jaw was still swollen, thanks to the pain meds and soft foods Chrissie had so thoughtfully provided before she lost her temper and stormed out, he called and left a message for Louise letting her know he'd be in tomorrow, as usual.

He wasn't looking forward to his first day back.

Monday Morning

Given how furious Chrissie had been with him when she left, he knew it would be awkward working with her today, but he hoped she wouldn't embarrass herself or him by making a scene. She'd had a couple of days to cool down; hopefully that would be enough.

When he arrived at work, there was a sign indicating everyone was to park out front and meet in the main building for a staff meeting. Unusual, but not unprecedented. Sometimes Louise held meetings to introduce new staff members, but he wasn't aware of any new hires.

His jaw was really stiff and sore, but they warned him it would be. They said warm compresses would help, so he stuffed the one they sent home with him into his backpack. He could zap it in the microwave in Evka's office as needed. If he felt worse, he could always just put in a half day and then go home, but he thought he'd be okay if he didn't do any heavy lifting. He'd let Louise know what his limitations were for the next few days.

When he went in, the smell of coffee and donuts made his knees weak. He would normally have had a Starbucks on the way in and kept his eco-friendly thermos full all day, but the surgeon was pretty adamant about not drinking any coffee for at least five days. Instead, he pulled his water bottle out from his backpack and took some cautious sips to stay hydrated.

They didn't say anything about donuts, though. He hadn't had solid food in two days. He was definitely hungry. He stacked a maple bar and an old-fashioned glazed onto a paper towel and returned to his seat. Chewing carefully on one side of his mouth, he successfully finished the old-fashioned and was starting in on the maple bar as people drifted in.

Kit teased him about his lumpy face, but said she'd help him out today if he needed it. Neil, looking rested from his vacation, nodded, then went to get coffee, then sat at the end of the row. Carrie came in next. She and Kim sat in front of him. Jimmy was unusually tired looking this morning and held up the wall in the back of the room. Several people came over to ask how his surgery went, then went to find a chair when they saw Louise come in.

IN PLAIN SIGHT

Taking a seat two rows up from his, Chrissie avoided looking in his direction, which was fine with him. He didn't see Evka, but maybe she had an emergency at the animal hospital. Logan, the wildlife hospital volunteer who worked with Evka, walked in wearing a particularly nice-fitting pair of jeans, her long, auburn hair loose around her shoulders. Normally, he would have waved her over or at least let her know he liked the way she looked in those jeans, but after what happened with Chrissie, decided to keep it in his pants today.

He really needed to keep his mind on work not women. If what Chrissie said about everyone knowing about his feelings for Evka . . . that was just plain embarrassing. And he had to admit that he must have sent the wrong signals to Chrissie. He liked women and he liked the back and forth of flirting with them. Women liked him. But obviously, something needed to change. What worked for him in his twenties wasn't working so well in his thirties. Maybe that's why Evka had walked away from a relationship with him. She probably thought he wasn't serious and couldn't be trusted. But he could! He'd have to show her he was boyfriend material, not just a user.

Just then, Louise came in and he could tell right away this was not going to be a normal staff meeting. No joking, no friendly small talk. All business. She started right in.

When Louise announced that Evka had been found dead on Friday, Aaron felt like he'd been suddenly drenched with a bucket of ice-cold water. He couldn't have heard Louise correctly. Evka wasn't dead, she just wasn't here yet. Evka couldn't be dead!

But finally, as she continued talking, it sunk in. He had a thousand questions but couldn't get his mouth to work to ask them. As people recovered from the shock, they started asking when and how this happened, what did she die of, etc., but Louise wasn't giving any specifics beyond the bare facts that Evka had been discovered dead in one of the wards Friday morning, and since the cause of death was not apparent, the police were investigating. Until they completed their investigation, she wasn't allowed to say much more and really didn't know much more than that.

Aaron was still sitting there staring at her when she ended the Q&A portion of the meeting and wrote the detective's number on the board.

Louise continued giving instructions, saying he and Kit would handle the resident raptors this morning, then asking Chrissie and Logan to stay and help with meal prep. When Louise mentioned Chrissie's name, it jolted Aaron back into the present.

Chrissie!

Thursday, Chrissie had been furious with him, but she had been even more furious with Evka. She left his place around four or five Thursday night. He wished he could remember the exact time. He had no idea where she went after that, but as angry and out of control as she was, he wouldn't put it past her to drive directly to the center to have it out with her perceived rival.

Everyone knew Evka often worked late. She was usually there until six or later, depending on her case load and sometimes she stayed all night or came in very early to nurse one of her patients.

Suddenly, Aaron was afraid to look at Chrissie directly, but he did pull out his phone and quietly enter the number Louise had written on the board for Detective Tate.

24

It was almost ten before Logan and Chrissie were gloved up and got started preparing food for the resident and hospital raptors. Chrissie still looked a little shaken, so Logan didn't try to engage her in conversation. In fact, the girl was so distracted, she miscalculated and bumped one of the trays with her hip, sending it clattering to the floor. Tears sprung from eyes, but when Logan didn't overreact or criticize her, she managed to pull herself together and clean up the mess.

Logan reminded herself how young Chrissie was. She'd probably never experienced the death of a coworker before. If she wanted to talk, Logan was there, but she wisely left that up to Chrissie. For the next hour, they communicated as needed about what meat each raptor was getting that day, but other than that, they worked in silence.

Logan was somewhat surprised at Chrissie's reaction. She didn't think she had been that close to the vet, or even liked her. She rarely saw them working together. Evka usually turned down her offers to help, although she never said why.

They were almost done arranging the meals on trays when Aaron and Kit, finished with their resident raptor rounds, arrived to help. Logan noticed Chrissie directed her communication to Kit, not Aaron, as she usually did. In fact, both Aaron and Chrissie seemed to be studiously avoiding each other, but that was probably just her imagination.

She checked her phone again for messages to see if Jean had heard anything yet from Brad, the Lane County ME. Nothing from Jean, but there was a short note from Sam. Said she found some things that might be interesting. She'd do a little more digging and let her know when she got back tonight.

Because of her investigative reporter background, Sam had taken on the task of gathering background information on the people at the center closest to Evka. Sam didn't exactly know what they were looking for, but they had to start somewhere.

As they had planned, Jean left early and drove back to Newport yesterday to try to talk with Mia before the police found out who she was and contacted her first. Hatfield Marine Science Center was open, but the woman who answered the phone only worked weekends and had no idea who Mia was. Said to try the office when it opened next week.

Being a local, with a brother as a commercial fisherman, Jean knew some of the kids who worked at Hatfield. She reached one of them at home and he verified that yes, Mia did work there, but she wasn't scheduled to come in again until Monday. He didn't know if she had worked Friday or not.

She called Sam and Logan to let them know she'd try again, but she wouldn't be able to get there until after office hours, and who knew when that would be. Mondays always went long.

Logan thought about it and decided she didn't want to wait that long. Also, she felt she should be the one to tell Mia about Evka's death. Mia should at least hear it from someone she had met—even if it was under emotionally charged circumstances. She would drive out this afternoon after they finished up here. She just hoped the cops hadn't beat her to the punch. She doubted they would be very tactful or gentle in their notification. And, in a strange way, she also hoped Mia had an alibi.

The warning scrawled on the white board demanding Evka back off didn't seem to be the words Mia would choose if she wanted her lover to acknowledge their relationship openly. But, then again, she was probably overthinking it. She'd just wait to see what her reaction was when she got there.

Hopefully, Mia wouldn't shoot the messenger.

2:30 P.M.

HATFIELD MARINE SCIENCE CENTER

NEWPORT, OR

After crossing over the bridge, Logan started watching for the Hatfield Marine Science Center. She was familiar with the center, but always missed the turnoff. Not knowing what Mia's work hours were, she had skipped lunch and drove the two hours back to Lincoln County straight through. She spotted the entrance, parked and went into the visitor's center.

She only had Mia's first name and the fact that she worked with the Stranded Marine Mammal research group. Luckily, the woman behind the counter ran her finger down a list of extensions taped under the counter, picked up the phone and punched in the numbers. She asked for Mia. Logan couldn't hear what was said on the other end.

"Yes, she has a friend here . . ." She turned to Logan, "What was your name again, dear?"

Logan couldn't think of a lie fast enough, so just gave her real name. If nothing else, Mia would be curious to know why she was here.

"Yes, Logan McKenna. Thank you, I'll let her know."

"Your friend is just coming back from the bay, but when she arrives, they'll send her up. Shouldn't be but just a few minutes. You're welcome to look around while you wait. We've got our resident giant Pacific octopus back!"

Logan appreciated the offer to look around for free but paid the three dollars. The docent pointed the way and gave an approving smile.

The water in the large tank was crystal clear, lined with a variety of stones and large, natural looking rocky structures into which the octopus could retreat when it got tired of being gawked at. Logan was delighted to see the large, rosy-brown octopus, its pale suckers all exposed, floating and stretching in full view, as if deciding what to do with her day. Fascinated, Logan watched as the graceful creature reached a few tentacles out and skillfully manipulated a large, blue plastic ball into a lime green tube and back out again. Octopus toys—who knew?

Mesmerized by this cephalopod theater, Logan didn't hear Mia come up behind her.

"What are you doing here?" Mia growled, her voice low.

Logan about jumped out of her skin but forced herself not to visibly react.

Well, at least she can't attack me here; there'd be witnesses.

"Hello, Mia," Logan said.

Mia did not look pleased to see her.

"I am sorry to come to where you work, but I didn't know your last name or where you lived. I had no other way to contact you," she said.

Arms crossed; Mia glared at her. "If this is about Evka, I have nothing to say to you. She already called and explained you two are just work friends. Was she lying?"

"This is about Evka, Mia," Logan said. "But no, Evka was not lying. We are just friends. Is there somewhere we can go and talk in private?"

Mia's brow furrowed, then she said, "We can go out here."

Following Mia outside, Logan zipped up her coat and pulled her hat and gloves out of her pocket and put them on. It was freezing, but at least it wasn't raining. They walked around the side of the building, out of the wind.

"Okay, what was so important you had to drive all the way over here and talk to me in person?"

Logan shoved her hands deeper into her pockets.

You're not going to make this easy, are you?

"Is there any place we can go inside and sit? This won't take long," Logan said.

"Unbelievable," Mia muttered, but walked across the parking lot to a small, low rectangular building. It was locked, but she pulled a key out from under a pot near the door. Inside it looked like an abandoned summer camp auditorium. Dusty, with a scattering of tables and chairs. One large window at the other end, but no electricity. At least, Mia didn't turn any on. Maybe it was a youth center. Several folding rectangular tables with attached benches were near the door. Mia sat on the end of one and pointed to the other side.

Logan looked at Mia's face. She had only seen her angry. In this light, sitting here patiently, she just looked tired. And her face looked softer. She had pretty, blue eyes.

Logan didn't want to be here. She didn't want to shatter this woman's world with the words she knew she needed to say.

When she finally got them out, the keening cry that emitted from Mia's breast was the worst sound Logan had ever heard. Instinctively, she went into mom mode and reached out to hold the grieving woman's hands in her own.

Sometimes that's all you can do.

25

After another wave of what appeared to be genuine, abject grief, Mia cried until she wore herself out, then asked a lot of questions, most of which Logan could not answer. Since they didn't know yet what the cause of death was or exactly what happened that night, all she could tell her was how they found her and that the police were investigating as if it were a homicide, just in case it was. She did not mention the trashed office. Even though Mia's grief seemed genuine, that didn't eliminate her from suspicion.

"Do you have any idea who may have wanted to harm Evka?" Logan asked. "Anyone at work, from the center?"

Mia wiped her eyes on her sweatshirt. "No," Mia said. "I mean, I never met any of them, but Evka never said she was afraid of anyone there."

"What about people she may have been involved with?" Logan asked. "I know this may be a sensitive topic, but the police will probably ask you the same thing . . ."

Mia straightened up in alarm. "The police? Are the police coming here?" Then she angrily stood. "Did you tell them about me?"

Logan quickly reassured her. "No, I haven't said anything to the police. I came here because I figured you wouldn't want to hear this kind of news from the police first."

Mia sat back down.

"Thank you," she said.

"But they're going to find out about you, if they haven't already," Logan said. "They'll have access to Evka's phone at some point, so they'll see all your calls and texts."

Mia groaned. "Those are personal!"

"Nothing's personal in a police investigation," Logan said. "Look, the best thing you can do is get some rest, start thinking through whatever kind of arrangements you want to make for a funeral or memorial service for Evka after they release her body. I'm not sure what the procedure is if there is no surviving family. Did Evka have a will? If she mentions you in that, maybe they'll release her to you."

"I don't know," Mia said.

"Will they do an autopsy?" she asked, her jaw clenched.

"Yes," Logan said. "That's standard procedure whenever the cause of death is unclear. My brother's a cop and Jean, my doctor friend I was telling you about who did the initial exam, is a Medical Examiner in Lincoln County."

Mia lowered her head into her hands. Logan waited until she was done with this round of crying, soft this time.

"The police will talk with everyone who was associated with Evka in any way. We've all been interviewed and I'm sure once they discover your relationship with Evka, they'll want to talk with you, too," Logan said. "When they do, you should be prepared. They'll want to know when you saw Evka last and where you were that night."

"I talked with her on the phone, but after I left her house that night I saw you—Wednesday—I drove back here, went to work, did my usual thing," Mia said.

"So you were at work here all day Thursday?" Logan asked. "What about Thursday night?"

"I stayed in. I was pretty wiped out from my argument with Evka."

"Did you order in a pizza? Try to think of anyone who may have seen you anytime Thursday night or early Friday morning."

She waited while Mia thought.

"No, I zapped a frozen dinner, had a beer, watched some TV, then went to bed early," she said.

Mia groaned and rubbed her face with her hands, then planted them firmly on her thighs. "And I can't account for Friday either. I was so upset I took Friday off. Stayed in bed. Channel surfed through daytime TV."

This wasn't good news for Mia. Logan believed her, but the police may not. In her experience, homicide detectives some-times stopped looking for other suspects once they found one with motive and opportunity—Eugene was only a two-and-a-half-hour drive from Newport— and Mia had no alibi.

"What about Evka's ex-husband?" Logan asked, "I know he's been out of the picture for a while and it didn't sound like their divorce was acrimonious, but do you know where he lives or where Evka might have his contact information? Even a last name would help."

"I don't know where he is," Mia said. "Last I heard, he went back to Australia. Maybe on her computer. I don't think they were in touch, but they could have been. We never talked about the past. I think his last name was Bangor or Banker, something like that."

"Well, news like this is completely draining and I'm sure you want some time alone," Logan said. "Just be ready for when the police get here and start asking questions."

She knew she had just done what was probably a very stupid thing. Whether Mia was guilty or not, what was to prevent her from running? That would not go over well with the two homicide detectives. She should at least find out where she lived.

"Do you need to go back into work, or can I give you a ride home? Are you staying someplace nearby? I have my car here," Logan said.

"No, there are housing facilities for students and visiting researchers in the back. Kind of a barracks area. I have an apartment to myself. I'm done for the day. I'll walk home from here."

"Okay," Logan said. "Let me put my number in your phone. My first husband was killed in a car accident a few years ago. I'll be happy to be a listening ear if you need one."

Mia handed her phone over and Logan quickly entered her number and handed it back.

Pocketing it, Mia got up, huffed out a deep breath, and blinked her eyes a few times to clear them from any remaining tears. "Thanks, that was very thoughtful of you. I'm sorry I gave you such a hard time that night. Evka and I had been fighting and then, there you were, sitting there in her house, looking better than I do on a good day . . . I just . . ."

"That's okay, Mia," Logan said. "I'm glad all that got straightened out. Evka and I were just friends."

"Yes, I know," Mia said. As they left the building, she turned and added, "But, it doesn't matter, now, does it?"

26

The adrenaline Logan had been running on the last few days since she discovered Evka's body finally ran out and left her feeling drained. Stumbling in from the drive back from Newport after delivering the sad news to Mia, Logan dropped her bag at the door to Jean's rental and saw a welcome sight.

Sam unpacking takeout from Mazatlán on the table. The aroma of warm tortillas and something spicy tempted her toward the food, but she held her hand up with all fingers spread and promised Sam she'd be back in five.

Peeling her clothes off in the hallway, Logan took a short, but very hot shower before coming back into the dining room to join Sam. She twisted her hair back into a scrunchie and reached for the chili verde. Mexican always did the trick. Logan scooped a generous portion onto her plate. For the next few minutes, both women focused on the food. When they came up for air, Sam told her Jean's window guy had called. He'd be there tomorrow between ten and two.

"Got it," Logan said, adding to the calendar on her phone.

Washing down the last of her shredded beef taco with a swig of beer, Sam pushed the takeout containers back and pulled over her computer.

"How'd Mia take the news?" Sam asked.

"Not well," Logan said.

"Think she was faking it?"

"If she was, she's a good actress," Logan said. "She seemed pretty busted up."

Logan laid her phone on the table and made sure the volume was up, so she'd hear it if Jean called. Jean was back at work today, but would call if her friend, Bart, the Lane County ME, got to Evka's autopsy today and had any news to share.

"Okay," Sam began. "While you were playing at the beach, I spent my morning getting to know the contestants on our 'people-closest-to-Evka' list. Pulled in some favors from a friend at the DMV and a state agency or two. Did the standard background search—property, tax liens, criminal records, lawsuits, that sort of thing. You'd be amazed at how much information there is about you in public records."

"Anything interesting?" Logan asked, getting up to get a beer. Sam already had one.

"Nothing earthshattering," Sam said. "I can't get into bank records, of course, and I didn't see any big red flags indicating financial difficulty or huge debt, but I did learn that Jimmy, our unassuming groundskeeper and all-around handyman, likes to gamble."

"How'd you find that out?" Logan asked.

Sam looked over her glasses, librarian style, at Logan. "I didn't ask, and my source didn't say, but I've used her before."

"Oh," Logan said, letting that one go.

Sam continued, "He says Jimmy sometimes pops over to Lucky Lil's, but more often, he drives up to Spirit Mountain about an hour and a half from Eugene at Grand Ronde."

"Okay," Logan said. "Not exactly a major crime. What else?"

She had a hard time picturing soft-spoken Jimmy as a heavy gambler, but you never knew what people got up to after work. And even if he was, how would that relate to Evka?

"No tax liens on any property that I could find. Most everyone rented. Only Louise, Neil, and Jimmy own property. Jimmy has a little mobile home on a scrap of land up from the center. Louise has a place not far in the other direction, and Neil owns a house just behind the event center. I found a few investment properties—a cabin in the mountains—a small rental in Old Town in Portland, but nothing in Evka's name.

"Chrissie sort of rents. She lives with her folks—well, not in the main house. She lives in a converted garage on the property. Same mailing address, though. I don't think it's a kosher build. No building permits or anything. A neighbor complained, that's why it's on record. Currently, it's unresolved with the city. They'll probably have to pay a big fine and unconvert it at some point. It's not zoned for that.

"Aaron rents a small house not far from here, and you've seen Evka's place. She's leased it for the last couple of years. Nice location backed onto the park like that. She could have had property somewhere else, but I can only check U.S. Records."

"Once we know more what we're looking for, I'll be able to focus my efforts, but I made short bios on a few key players."

"Yep, I'm ready—shoot. Who have you got?" Logan said.

"One personal connection, Mia, and the four co-workers and volunteers she spent the most time with." Sam said. "Let's start with Mia."

"Mia Schuster, forty-three years old, American. Born in Wisconsin. Large farm family. Changed high schools her senior year. Her address changed. Looks like she lived with another family that year. Social services was involved briefly, but no formal file was created. Don't know why. Maybe her high school records would have some notes, but those are confidential, and I don't have contacts there."

Logan made a mental note to call Huey. She'd met him through her consulting work with Fractals and since then had become good friends with him and his sister, Thanh, a talented Vietnamese chef in Portland. A straight up guy who also happened to be a skillful hacker, Huey's expertise had helped her decode information hidden on a flash drive that helped track down an abusive husband and helped uncover a killer.

27

"Mia was the oldest. Never married. BA and PhD in Wildlife Biology. Did her dissertation on the sable antelope. Met and worked with Evka in Africa at the Kenyan Game Reserve. Mia landed a spot on a research team conducting a study at Hatfield in Newport in September—a one-year stranded marine mammals study. She'll be out of a job in September."

"Yes, that fits with what they both told me," Logan said. "She said she and Evka were working things out, but from what Evka told me, that sounds like wishful thinking on Mia's part."

"Anything else on Mia?" Sam asked.

"No," Logan said. "Oh, wait. If we're covering all of Evka's personal connections, we should take a look at her ex-husband, Tim. Don't know his last name for sure, but Mia said it was Bangor or Banker—something like that."

Sam entered that information into her spreadsheet. "Was he back in the picture?"

"I don't think so," Logan said.

"Did she say where he is, now?"

"Somewhere in Australia—unless he's moved since then or come here. Evka told me they met in vet school in Sydney. She said they married in Kenya, but he didn't like Africa and went back to Australia when they divorced."

"Did they split up over Mia?"

"No, she met Mia after he left. Says the divorce was amicable. Not a volatile relationship—according to her," Logan said.

While Sam was finishing her notes on Evka's ex, Logan went to the kitchen and got a trash bag for the fast-food containers. All the good stuff was gone, but she spooned the rice and beans together in one box and popped it in the fridge. Leftovers made a great midnight snack.

Sam was ready when she got back.

"Okay. Next up, Nina Waverly, Evka's veterinary assistant, thirty-one, lives with her fiancé in an apartment near the university. He's a grad student. Business and accounting. They're into the environment, share an old truck, both have bikes. He rides his to school. Truck's registered in her name. Needs one to get around. She has two jobs plus school. She'd never make her connections taking the bus."

"I've met Nina, but we never work the same shifts. Gave Evka better coverage, I think. I knew she was in grad school. Wanted to become a vet. Where else does she work?"

"Eugene Animal Clinic, small office, only two vets, Drs. Patel and Harris. She works Mondays and Wednesday afternoons. Fairly recent hire at the Cascades Raptor Center, where she works Tuesdays and Thursdays. On top of all that, she's juggling a full course load."

No wonder Sam had earned awards as an investigative journalist. With contacts up and down the state, Sam was very good at her job. It didn't hurt that she lied as easily as other people breathed. To gather the information on Nina, she'd called the animal clinic, told them she was new in town and wanted to find a good vet. She invented a fictional feline fur baby named Marmalade and a brother in vet school. By the time she hung up, she and Nina were chatting like old pals and had agreed to meet for lunch sometime soon.

"You're amazing, you know that?" Logan said.

Sam smiled, accepting the praise as her due and pushed her glasses back up on her nose. Scanning her computer screen, she got back to it.

"Up next—Aaron, Chrissie, Neil, and Jimmy," she said. "When we finish with each one, we'll add follow up questions."

"Jean called yet?" she added.

Logan checked her phone, "Nope."

Sam read the first name.

"Aaron Whitlock, thirty-two. Lives at 4892 Fox Hollow Road, Apt 32D. Has roommates off and on, none right now. Born second to the youngest child of four to Jim and Betsy Whitlock of Fort Collins, Colorado. Stayed local, got good grades at Colorado State, graduated, then spent a few years bumming around South America before being accepted to grad school here in Eugene at UofO. Got his master's degree and was hired right out of grad school at the Cascades Raptor Center. His bio said he wanted to work with wild animals, raptors in particular, ever since he saw one as part of a school assembly in elementary school. Has worked here ever since he left U of O. No trouble with the law—at least not here."

28

S am continued with her report on Aaron.

"Never married. Dates, but no serious girlfriends in the last few years as far as anyone knows."

Logan felt a twinge of guilt gathering sensitive, personal information about these people who may have nothing to do with Evka's death, but on the other hand, someone had killed Evka, she was sure of it. And that someone needed to be held accountable.

She filled Sam in on her impression that Aaron liked the vet, but she added truthfully that she wasn't sure this had anything to do with anything. She had no knowledge of him ever acting on his feelings, how long he'd had them, or how Evka felt about it if she was aware of how he felt. They could have been having a raging affair for all she knew. Not sure how Mia fit into that, though. Confusing, but people led complicated lives. Who was she to judge?

Sam forged ahead.

"Chrissie Virtanen— started as a volunteer at the center, now works twenty hours a week while attending Lane Community College, also part time. Before she was hired at the Cascades Raptor Center, she worked part time in her mother's at-home daycare business. Flexible hours suited her school schedule. Lives on the property in a converted garage apartment—as we've already covered. You work with Chrissie—what else do we know about her?"

"Cheerful . . . young . . . passionate about the environment . . . and has a major crush on Aaron, speaking of crushes."

"But he liked Evka, right?" Sam asked.

"Well, yeah, but remember, I'm just basing this on the way Aaron was looking at Evka and Chrissie was looking at Aaron during that first orientation meeting at the center. None of them were seeing each other as far as I know, and I can't imagine emotions running high enough to lead to murder," Logan said. "Everyone gets crushes at work."

"This is just a brain dump, Logan," Sam said. "We'll sort through it later. For now, don't leave anything out. It all goes in."

Logan continued.

"Chrissie wants to be a trainer, but from the little I observed, Evka didn't seem to encourage that. Evka had that natural gift to work with raptors—a calmness and confidence. Aaron, too, and Kit, the bird curator. I'd say Chrissie has more enthusiasm than competence—she's kind of all over the map emotionally—sometimes over-the-top happy, other times slinks around in a bad mood. But she's young, hard to say how she'll turn out. Came in late a couple times, hung over, but I don't think anyone ratted her out, because Louise didn't mention it and I get the impression she wouldn't have tolerated that."

"What *did* Louise have to say about her?" Sam asked.

"Not much, just that she was bubbly, good with the public and competent, just not as naturally intuitive with the animals as some of the others. Solid C student, would probably never rise to any position of responsibility there."

"Okay, that brings us to Neil Matthew Baker. Sixty-three. Started out part time helping the groundskeeper, volunteered with the raptors, then got hired full time. He's done just about every job here except vet or director. Worked here forty-one years!"

"Wow," Logan said.

"Yeah, Louise said she hired him when he was still in college. Steady employee. Reliable. Can do most every job here but prefers to remain a trainer. Lives over on Adams Street, behind the event center, in the house he grew up in. His mom died years ago. Worked with all of the others but wasn't particularly close to any of them. Does that sound about right?"

Logan nodded. "Yep, he knows his stuff, but doesn't socialize with anyone. He and Aaron showed me the ropes when I first got here."

"Moving on, last but not least, James Townsend—Jimmy to everyone here. Seventy-two years old . . ."

"Seventy-two? Really?" Logan said. "He looks younger than that."

She remembered how kind the man had been to her when she first arrived. With old-fashioned manners, he'd bent his tall frame down and extended his hand to help her out of her car, smiling from under his cap. Evka always offered him coffee when he came around. He even had his own mug, a green one with the face of a great horned owl on it.

"Jimmy's been employed at the center for twenty-five years—second only to Neil in long term employment. And Louise, of course, the founder. What an amazing woman! She had a vision and made it happen. Anyway, Jimmy worked construction in the Eugene area before that until it got too tough on his back.

"Born in the south . . . Louise said one of his parents taught college, but he never went to college himself. Got shipped off to Vietnam right out of high school. Did two tours of duty as a medic. Came back home to Oregon."

"I wonder why he didn't become an EMT or a fire fighter or go into the medical field," Logan said. "With the GI Bill and that medical background, he'd have a leg up."

"Don't know," Sam said. "But he's lived a quiet life here. Maybe he wanted to get away from any memories of the war."

"Yeah, Louise says he's a gem. Moves slow, but smart and gets the job done.'

Sam paused.

Logan picked up on her hesitation right away. "What else did you find?"

"Nothing that really applies to this—nothing to do with Evka, but there are some rotten apples on Jimmy's family tree. His father moved the family to Oregon from Louisiana not long after Jimmy was born. I was curious, so I did some digging. Couple of cousins have lengthy criminal records. One of his brothers is serving time in Tennessee for murder. Attached to one of the more violent prison gangs. They're equal opportunity haters. Foreigners, immigrants, people of any color except white."

"Wow," Logan said. "I can see his southern gentleman roots—opens doors and tips his hat—but I can't see Jimmy being involved with any of the rest of that."

"I sure hope not," Sam said. She scrolled down to see more of her screen.

"Last but not least, our director, Louise Shimmel," Sam said. "Brilliant, powerful fundraiser, passionate about raptors. Started rehabilitating rescued wildlife out of her home and somehow negotiated and purchased a tract of land on Fox Hollow Road from the City of Eugene. Says here she started with twelve resident education birds and built it over the years to forty resident birds. They treat over seven hundred wild patients every year. Impressive."

"Now," Sam said. "You worked with these people. Did they all get along with Evka? Any outside of work personal connections, any red flags?"

"Louise hired Evka a couple of years ago," Logan said. "They had a good working relationship, but I don't think they socialized after hours. As for Neil, I don't think he socialized with anyone, either, outside of work."

"What about Aaron, Chrissie, Jimmy, or her assistant?"

"I did notice during orientation that Chrissie had a crush on Aaron and Aaron was paying a lot of attention to Evka, but none of them had a relationship outside of the center that I know of, other than the usual go get pizza after work or Christmas party deals."

"Yeah, but you never know what happens after work. If Aaron and Evka were involved, and Aaron found out about Mia . . . that could be trouble."

Sam sat back in her chair and pushed her glasses up again.

Logan closed her laptop and checked her phone to see if Jean called. She'd had it on mute when she was talking with Mia. No missed call, but there was a text. She shared it with Sam.

"Jean says she's still with patients but will call as soon as she hears from her friend, Bart," Logan said.

"Do you really think Evka was murdered?" Sam asked. "Don't get me wrong, I'm all in until our resident dead body expert tells us otherwise, but I sure wish we had something definitive to go on."

Logan sat back in her chair and looked out the window. This could all just be a waste of time. Evka could have just had a heart attack or something. No one knew her well. Maybe she had some other health issue that wasn't apparent. She thought back to her discovery of Evka's body. She'd opened the door and . . .

"That's it!" she said. "Probably not enough to pass muster with the police, but the light was out!"

"What light?" Sam asked.

"Ward 3!" Logan said. "When I rushed in to see if Evka was still breathing, I switched on the light."

Sam still looked blank.

"If Evka was working in ward 3, she would have had the light on. And if she died of natural causes, the light would still have been on when I found her the next morning. She couldn't have turned it off herself if she died of a heart attack. So . . ."

Logan looked at Sam expectantly.

"Who turned out the light?"

29

It was past dark when Jean called. As she predicted, it had been a busy Monday. She had been swamped all day with her regular medical practice and was now on her way home, driving south on the 101 to Newport. But she had spoken with the Lane County ME and wanted to give them a report before she got home. She and her husband had a no-tech policy at dinner.

Logan put her on speaker.

"I wish I had something more substantial to report," Jean said. "Bart did the autopsy today, but he says it's a nothing burger. No signs of a struggle, no wounds except a bump on her head from falling on the floor. He thinks it looks like natural causes, probably a heart attack."

Logan's heart fell. She was hoping he'd find something. Something that explained the violence done to Evka's office and the threatening message left on the whiteboard.

"Is that what he's putting on the report? What about the office being trashed? Are they just going to ignore that?"

"Bart's job is to report medical findings," Jean said.

Logan let out an exasperated sigh. Jean was right, but she didn't like it. Neither did Sam. She butted into the conversation.

"He has some discretion, right?" Sam said.

"Hang on," Jean said. "Don't get your panties in a wad. Bart's a professional. And he's careful. He's holding off on filling in the cause-of-death box until he's sure. He's sending off for a tox screen, but if it comes back negative, he'll have to go with natural causes. All signs point to a heart attack."

"If they find some kind of poison, that means she was killed, right? She wouldn't be stupid enough to accidentally poison herself," said Logan.

"Let's wait for the tox results," Jean said.

"And how long will those take?" Logan asked.

"Depends, but even with a rush, it can take two or three weeks. Usually it's four to six," she said. "When the cops wrap up their investigation, that's it."

While they were talking, Logan turned the gas fireplace on. She and Sam migrated to the living room.

"Any idea how that's going?" Logan asked. "The investigation? How well does Bart know those two detectives . . . Tate and . . . ?"

"Voss, Tate and Voss," Sam supplied.

"Yeah, he knows them pretty well, he's worked with them in other cases, although Eugene isn't really a hotbed of murders," Jean said. "They may only have four to five a year, max."

Sam signed an impatient 'let's-move-this-along' rolling motions with her hand.

"So what does Bart know about their investigation?" Logan prodded.

"He says it's still open. They're working through interviewing everyone, canvassing the neighborhood, looking for CCTV footage, checking schedules, and processing fingerprints found in Evka's office and in the room where she was found—eliminating the ones that would show up from people who worked there," Jean said.

"But whoever killed Evka was probably someone who worked closely with her," Logan said. "So how does that help?"

"*If* she was killed," Jean said. "They have to start somewhere. It's a slow process."

Jean had nothing else to report, so she reminded Logan that the window guy was coming tomorrow and the company doing the counter for the half bath would fit them in Thursday. Before she got off the phone, she said she would let them know when Bart called back with the toxicology results but warned them again that it would be a while.

Sam continued to click away at her keyboard, intent on her laptop screen, no doubt itching to write her notes into a story. Hopefully, since this incident happened in Eugene, it would be out of reporting zone for the News Times, but she might be able to sell it as a freelancer. Logan wasn't sure how that worked. She hoped Sam would wait to pull the trigger on any story until they knew more. She'd have to make her pinkie swear.

Sam must have read her mind. She kept her fingertips hovering over the keyboard and looked Logan straight in the eye.

"Don't worry, Logan," she said. "If there's a story here, I'll write it, but right now, our main priority is to find whoever did this. For what it's worth, I don't think it was a natural death. My nose is itching—and my nose is never wrong. I think it was murder."

Logan agreed. Since there was nothing else they could do tonight, they decided to take a break from playing cop and watch some escapist TV. Jean had WIFI and a sixty-inch television mounted on the wall to the left of the fireplace. Logan let Sam choose the show, so for the next hour, she watched as a female vampire sank her teeth into a handsome if clueless mortal, then after she dominatrixed him, took on a whole town of zombies.

Okay, then . . .

She and Sam were definitely from different generations. Logan preferred *Hunt for Red October*, Alfred Hitchcock's *Rear Window*, or even *Silence of the Lambs*. Suspense, psychological drama versus one long chase scene or fifteen dead bodies in the first fifteen minutes.

After Sam went to bed, Logan poured herself half a glass of merlot and called Ben. It was good to hear his voice. She caught him up on what was happening here, then insisted he share his day with her. She wanted to hear about normal things. Things that had nothing to do with murder—or vampires and zombies for that matter.

Later, lying in bed, her mind drifted back to Evka and the real-life mystery she, Sam, and Jean were trying to unravel. Just as she started to drift off, her eyes flew open.

The phone. She'd forgotten to ask Jean if Bart said anything about Evka's phone. If they'd found it or not. She'd never seen Evka without it and it was nowhere to be seen in ward 3. They needed to know who Evka was in contact with that night. And before. Her phone would tell a much more complete story than the basic information they'd been able to collect so far.

Who did Evka talk with? And when?

She'd have to add it to the things she wanted Huey to track down. His first class started at 9:00 a.m., but he was usually in before that. She'd call first thing in the morning. She didn't have the physical phone, but she had Evka's number. She hoped that was enough. Of course, they should have a warrant, but if it was for a good cause, she knew Huey would break some rules for her. She was counting on it.

She burrowed into the covers. Knowing she had a lead to follow, something to track down instead of just waiting for the police to figure things out, made her feel much better. The truth was there. She just had to find it.

30

Detective Tate was frustrated.

Saturday they'd gone back several times to complete the canvassing of the neighborhood near the Cascades Raptor Center. There was only one homeowner they'd been unable to reach, a Mr. Gary Zimmerman. So far homeowners either didn't have security cameras, or they were only aimed at front porches to catch package thieves.

This morning they tried again. No luck, but a neighbor came out and told them Zimmerman's wife had been rushed to the hospital Friday night. She'd been battling inoperable brain cancer for months and was losing the battle. Her husband had been with her all weekend.

Punching in the number the neighbor gave him for the man's cell, Detective Tate listened as it rang twice then went to voicemail. He left a short message asking him to return the call as soon as possible.

He almost drove down to the hospital, but since they weren't even sure this was a homicide, he didn't want to intrude on what may be Zimmerman's last few hours with his wife.

So he sent Voss home and spent most of the day at his desk going over the interviews they had been able to conduct. They'd run the fingerprints they had through AFIS, but the only hits were employees at the center whose prints would have been found there naturally.

Around four o'clock he looked at the clock and rubbed his face, then reached for the phone and waited for someone to pick up.

He and his wife were both in good health—no brain cancer anyway—but if there's one thing this job had taught him, it's that no one is promised a tomorrow.

"Carmichaels, how can I help you?" a cheerful woman intoned.

"Do you have any reservations left for two tonight?"

MONDAY, FEBRUARY 28

Feeling guilty for having taken the night off, Tate felt a brief stab of anxiety, a familiar kick in the gut he got when a case had gone more than forty-eight hours without resolution. Like the white rabbit running against time, but unable to do anything about it without more information.

When Voss came in, Tate glowered at him.

"Well, good Monday morning to you, too, Sunshine," Voss said, taking off his jacket and sitting down across from him. Their desks faced each other.

"Sorry," said Tate.

For the rest of the morning, they went over the interviews they had—with the vet assistant, a vendor who delivered live chicks, and every other person they'd talked with. Then they moved on to the copies of the personnel files the director of the center had shared with them on Friday. They had just started in on the report from the crime scene techs of the vet's vandalized office when the phone rang.

It was Bart.

Tate put him on speaker.

"As you know, this is just preliminary, but I knew you were waiting on this, so wanted to call before I wrote up my results," Bart said.

"Well?" said Voss.

Bart cut right to the chase. "No signs it was homicide."

Voss groaned and Tate squeezed his eyes shut. *Fuck.* He'd been counting on something breaking. "So natural causes?" he said in a dispirited tone.

"You didn't let me finish," Bart said. "There was nothing to indicate a struggle, no wounds that couldn't be accounted for by falling to the floor, but I'm not ready to call this one a heart attack, yet. I've sent off for toxicology. And before you ask, yes, I put a rush on it. Hopefully in a couple of weeks."

"Until then?" Voss asked. He had less experience with homicide than Tate.

"Until then Ms. Novatna will remain a guest of Lane County at Ferrel's Mortuary," Bart said.

"Which means we get back to work," Tate said.

They broke for a quick lunch. When they returned, one of the crime scene techs popped her head in the door.

"You guys got a minute?"

"Sure, what's up?" Tate said.

"I was writing up the report on everything we collected at the Cascades Raptor Center Friday, and something stood out. Wanted to run it by you guys. See if it meant anything."

"Shoot," said Tate.

"The message on the whiteboard was written with a red marker. There were two red markers at the scene. The one in the top desk drawer had the vet's prints on it and a few smudged ones we couldn't identify. The other one—the one on the floor near the tray—looked relatively new and had only had one set of prints . . ."

"And?" Voss said.

"They belonged to a Christine Vertanen. Don't know if it has anything to do with your DB, but it sure points the finger at her being the one who trashed that office," the tech said.

Tate didn't know either, but he was glad to have a lead—any lead. He thanked the tech for her attention to detail then looked up the address. At the very least, they needed to know if she had an alibi and what grudge she may have had against the vet. What did she want her to 'back off' from?

They found the girl at home, between classes. Her mother wanted to stay with her daughter, but Chrissie, as she preferred to be called, was no longer a minor, so they sat down with her in her converted garage apartment. They Mirandized her, but so far, Chrissie hadn't asked for a lawyer.

"Nice place you've got here," Tate began, trying to sound sincere.

Even with the space heater, the place was freezing. They'd put down carpet, but the cold seeped up through the concrete floor and he doubted it was insulated. He hadn't lived like this since college, but knew that to someone Chrissie's age, having your own place, even if it came with paper thin walls and was within a stone's throw of your parents' house, was desirable. Especially if it was rent free.

"Thanks," Chrissie said.

There were only two chairs at the little dinette table, so Voss leaned against the makeshift kitchen counter near the sink while Tate sat across from Chrissie.

Their person of interest looked very nervous.

31

"**A**s we said before, I'm Detective Tate and this is Detective Voss," he said, placing his phone on the table between them. "You don't mind if I record our conversation, do you?"

Chrissie shook her head and folded her hands in her lap. After stating the date and the people present, Tate got started.

"We just need to ask you a few questions about what happened Thursday night and Friday morning at the Cascades Raptor Center. We're establishing a timeline with everyone. You work there part time, is that right?"

"Yes," Chrissie answered, glad they weren't asking any difficult questions. "My schedule varies depending on my courses each semester, but I usually work about twenty hours a week."

"What do you do there?" Tate sounded genuinely interested.

Chrissie leaned forward, warming to the task. "Oh, I do just about everything. I help take care of the raptors, of course, but I'm working on becoming a trainer soon. I already help the trainers. I know how to do it all, I just need the certificate. I'm very good with the raptors."

"I'm sure you are, Chrissie," Tate said. "So in the course of your duties at the center, you must have worked closely with the vet, Evka Novatna, the woman who died, right?"

Chrissie stiffened. "Well, not really. I mean, yes, sometimes, but not a lot. I could have helped her more, but she didn't really . . . well, I worked in other areas of the center more often. I worked on the resident raptors team. Everyone requests me. The trainers are always asking for my help."

"Okay, we don't want to take up too much of your time, Chrissie," Tate said. "We'll get back to your relationship with the vet later, but for now, can you tell us where you were from Thursday night through Friday morning when Ms. Novatna's body was discovered?"

This was not an area Chrissie wanted to get into. She'd have to tell them about Aaron. There was nothing wrong with her helping a coworker out. She just hoped they didn't verify her story by talking with him. He might blab about their fight at his place.

"Thursday . . . let me think," she said, striving for a casual tone. "Oh yeah, I gave a friend a ride home from his dentist office. He had a couple of wisdom teeth pulled."

"Which coworker?" Tate said.

"Um, Aaron, Aaron Whitlock," she said. "He's one of the trainers."

"And what time was that?"

"Oh, I don't remember exactly," she said. "Maybe late afternoon?"

"Can you be any more precise?" he said. "Maybe you can give Aaron a call and ask him?"

No, I couldn't. She was pretty sure Aaron wouldn't take her call and then they'd start asking questions.

"I think it was around 5:00," she said. "Yes, it was definitely 5:00. I remember because it took a while to get home. There was a lot of traffic."

"So you got home around what? 5:30? What did you do after that?"

"Oh, I didn't go home right away," she said. "I stopped and had dinner, then went home."

"Where was that?"

"Just a local place nearby," she said. "Lone Star—they have good burgers."

"I'll have to try that sometime. We like burgers, don't we Voss?"

"Always," Voss said.

"What time did you leave Lone Star?"

"Around seven," Chrissie said.

"Long time to eat dinner," Tate said.

"They must have been busy," she said. "It took a while to get my food."

She didn't mention the two beers she put away with her burger and the two she had after.

"So then you went home," he said.

"Yes," she said, relaxing her posture a little.

"What did you do next?" he asked.

"Nothing," she said. "I went to bed early."

"What about Friday?"

"I slept in," she said. "I don't work Fridays. My first class wasn't until two. I didn't find out about what happened until Monday."

"Can anyone verify that, Chrissie?" Tate asked.

"I went over and helped my mom for an hour around noon to feed the daycare kids lunch—things get pretty busy for her. I made lunch for the older ones while she put the two in diapers down for their nap."

"So you were home from 7:00 p.m. Thursday night until noon Friday, is that right?" Tate asked.

"Yes, that sounds about right," Chrissie answered. *It was almost over! They'd be leaving soon.*

Tate leaned back, lifting the front legs of his chair off the floor, drilling her with a dead-eye stare.

"Then how do you explain your fingerprints being the only ones found on the red marker used to write the threatening message to the vet—and then trash her office? It's time to talk about what your real relationship was with Evka Novatna. We're going to go back and start over. And this time, we want the truth. All of it."

*****

Within minutes, Chrissie folded. Through sobs and tears, she confessed to vandalizing Evka's office, even writing the threatening message, but she insisted she had nothing to do with the vet's death.

"She was a cougar! She got her claws into Aaron!" she said. "I just wanted her to leave him alone—that's all! Just wanted her to back off! I wasn't going to *do* anything!"

"So you admit to being in her office that morning, Friday, sometime after four o'clock?" Tate said. "And you didn't see Evka at all?"

"No," Chrissie said. "I must have just missed her. I went by her house first, but she wasn't there."

"Didn't you see her car?"

"No, Evka parks in back and the front gate was locked as usual, so I parked on the street and walked in," she said. "When I didn't see her, I thought maybe she was on her way home. I swear I never saw her!"

A fresh wave of crying began. "This is so messed up! I only wanted to talk to her. Tell her to stay away from Aaron. Everything was fine until she came along."

Tate handed her a tissue. While he was waiting, deciding whether or not to take her in for vandalism and try to squeeze more information out of her back at the station, his cell burred. It was the phone company. Evka's phone records.

He paused the recording and scrolled through the list of Evka's texts and calls, scanning as he went. Then, he stood up and handed a very surprised Chrissie his card, giving her the usual spiel about not leaving town, abruptly terminating their interview.

Once they were in the car Voss turned to Tate and said, "What was that about? She just confessed! I thought we were taking her in."

In response, Tate showed him the densely packed message he'd just received.

"Wow," Voss said. "Definitely a double espresso job. Can we swing by Jammy Java's?

32

Back at the station, Tate printed everything out while Voss commandeered a small conference table where they could spread it all out.

Before they could even begin to see what they had, Tate's cell rang. It was from Zimmerman, the man from 1422 Fox Hollow Road, five houses down from the center. The man whose wife was in the hospital.

"Hello, Tate here," he said.

"Detective Tate, this is Rob Zimmerman. I'm sorry it's taken me a few days to get back to you," he said. "My wife has been ill."

"Yes, we heard," Tate said. "How is your wife doing?"

"Not good, but they've got her stable—again," he said. "At least for a while."

Zimmerman's voice broke and Tate waited for him to regain control.

"In the message you left, you said you were looking for anyone who had security cameras, video of our street?"

"Yes," Tate said. "Detective Voss and I are following up on an incident that occurred at the Cascades Raptor Center sometime Thursday night or very early Friday morning."

"The hawk place?" Rob said. "What happened? Did someone try to steal one of the birds?"

"No, sir," Tate said. "We know you were not present at that time, but we are asking anyone who may have security cameras that reached the street to share that video with us. It will help us wrap up this investigation and finalize our report. We're particularly interested in Thursday and Friday."

"Of course," Rob said. "We had a break in last year, so I got a pretty good system installed. If everything's working, it should still have video from those nights. I'm home now, you're welcome to come by anytime, but can we make it quick? I'm wiped out. Gonna take a shower—got a few things to take care of here. A neighbor's watching our dog. I need to be back at the hospital in a couple of hours . . . .they don't know how much longer she . . ."

"I understand, sir," Tate said. "Thank you for helping us out. We'll leave now. Be there in twenty minutes."

"Okay," he said. "I'll wait, but if the hospital calls . . ."

"Yes, of course," Tate said.

*****

Once there, Tate and Voss got right to the point. They wanted to take as little of the man's time as possible. They collected the SIM card and left the distraught husband in peace. Both were glad they were not in his shoes. Voss wasn't married and Tate couldn't imagine life without his wife. He pushed the thought out of his mind.

When they got back to their desks, they uploaded the footage and settled in to take a look at what they had, see how it lined up with the phone records. Voss had pulled the DMV records for Evka and the three people she communicated with that night.

IN PLAIN SIGHT

Mr. Zimmerman's camera captured video from 5:00 p.m. Thursday evening until 5:00 p.m. Friday. Since he was at the hospital with his wife, he wasn't home after that to reset it as he usually did. But that was okay because this was the time period they needed.

Tate grabbed a uniform to help, but even then, it was going to take a while to go through it all. They had to zoom in on every vehicle that passed in the first few hours, track down each license plate. Most of the cars driving by the Zimmerman home belonged to residents on the street returning from work, going out to dinner, etc. The street wasn't a main thoroughfare, so there were only a few vehicles that didn't belong to someone who lived on Fox Hollow or nearby.

Of the vehicles belonging to Cascades Raptor Center employees, most came and went as expected, according to their owners' statements. The director, the vet's assistant, two trainers and a volunteer all left after work and did not return that night or before five Friday morning.

As the time stamp progressed, traffic reduced to a trickle. A beat-up black Silverado 150 came into view at 12:16 a.m. Tate had Voss pause the tape and checked the license plate number. They had a match. But it wasn't Chrissie's vehicle. It was registered to the groundskeeper's, Jimmy Townsend.

"Well, well, well . . ." Tate said.

"Unless Mr. Townsend was putting in overtime," Voss said. "I'd say he's got some *'splaining* to do."

It was coming up on five o'clock and they still had to watch the rest of the video footage, corroborate Chrissie's story, and then go through Evka's phone records. He needed to see who Evka had communicated with that week—Thursday and Friday in particular. Maybe something would shake loose.

Tate sent the uniform home, then put a call in to his wife while Voss ordered pizza.

On Tuesday. they drove down to the Cascades Raptor Center to find Jimmy. Calling first would have put the groundskeeper on alert and they wanted to catch him off guard, so they just dropped in. They didn't have to look very hard; Jimmy was working on the front gate when they drove in. He stood to one side and watched as they parked and got out of their car.

"Mr. Townsend," Tate said, reaching out to shake his hand. "If you have a few minutes, my partner and I have a few more questions to ask you regarding last week's events. It will just take a few minutes."

"Sure," Jimmy said. "Let me tie this back so it won't hit anybody's car until I can get back to it. Spring wore out."

He led them back to his workshop and again offered them the only two chairs in the place. Tate took one and gestured for him to take the other. Voss remained standing near the doorway, as if Jimmy might try to escape. The vote was still out on that.

Tate got right to the point, asking if he owned a black Silverado 150, giving him the license plate number. Jimmy verified that was his truck.

"What's this all about?"

"Your truck was seen on Fox Hollow Thursday night around midnight. Can you tell us about that? Why you would be at the center that late?" Tate asked.

Jimmy rubbed the palms of his hands on his jeans, then said, "Well, yes, I was here that night."

Tate waited for him to continue. Silence was one of his most powerful interviewing tools. Suspects always filled the gap.

"I came to give Evka some good news. I'd been up to Spirit Mountain, and I won. I won big enough to help her out. She wanted to go in with Louise—help expand the center. Enlarge it so they could help more raptors. Every year the number of animals that need rescuing keeps going up. We can't handle them all with what we have now. It probably would have been a loan, but I wouldn't have charged them any interest."

Tate looked doubtful.

"That's the God's honest truth," Jimmy said. "Evka already offered to pay me back. Said she had some money coming in soon."

"Why didn't you tell us this before?" Voss asked.

"Well, for obvious reasons, because of what happened," Jimmy said. "I came in, like I said, shared the news with Evka, then I left to go home and catch a few hours' sleep. I had to work the next day."

"Evka was fine when I left," he said. "And her office was fine, too. Nothing looked out of place and no one else was here. Everything that happened, happened after I left."

Tate still didn't seem satisfied, but he had no physical evidence to tie Jimmy to the murder itself, so he warned him not to leave town and said they'd probably talk with him again soon. Then he and Voss left and drove back to the station.

Maybe there was something in Jimmy's phone records that would help.

Given that they could place his black Silverado 150 driving down the street in front of the Cascades Raptor Center the night their victim was killed, Tate was confident the judge would sign off on a warrant for Townsend's phone records. She did.

33

Logan skimmed the surface of a shallow sleep until about six, then got up and dressed in the diffuse light of a gray dawn. Following her nose to the kitchen, she was grateful Sam had programmed the coffee maker the night before. Ben was working on a remote site this week. She filled a mug and gave him a call. She needed to hear his voice. He picked up on the second ring.

As she listened, Logan looked out the dining room window at the low-slung clouds hanging in a sharkskin sky. The hummingbird feeder had no customers. March was slinking in more like a mouse than a lion. But in talking with Ben, Logan felt her energy returning. Not only did he brighten her morning, but when she lay everything out to him, she realized she didn't have to sit around waiting. By the time she hung up, she realized there were at least two proactive things she could do.

First, a text had come in while she was on the phone with Ben. It was Louise, asking if she wanted to sit in on the necropsy of the red-tailed hawk. Doing an autopsy on a raptor was to be part of her volunteer training, anyway. Logan immediately accepted. It was scheduled for 10:00 a.m. tomorrow. If the examination revealed the death of the red tail was caused by a human, not the result of a panicked flight around the exam room, then the police would have to consider Evka's death a homicide. It was doubtful Evka killed her own patient. Another box to check.

Second, she called Huey. When she'd explained what she needed and why, he was more than happy to help. Obtaining Evka's phone records he could do, but she'd have to come get the printout of the records in person. Faxing, forwarding, or attaching them to an email would leave a trail the police could easily follow should they ever decide to track his technology activities. Logan was fine with that. It was time for a road trip anyway. Huey said he could probably have it ready by that night.

WEDNESDAY, MARCH 2

10:00 A.M.

CASCADES RAPTOR CENTER

Logan arrived at the animal hospital as Louise was bringing the dead red tail out of the refrigerator where it had been kept since its discovery Friday. Just seeing the magnificent animal reduced to a bundle of lifeless bone and feathers on the cold, steel table made her heart ache. She got out her notebook and began to take notes as Louise spoke.

"*Buteo jamaicensis* . . . two-year-old male . . . Fractured skull, broken right wing . . ."

Although the necropsy was fascinating and Logan learned a lot, Louise could only determine that the hawk had died of its injuries and probably acute stress. There was no way to tell for sure if a human had done any of the damage or if the hawk's death was the result of a tragic, panicked flight crashing into walls, ending in a heap on the floor.

After she helped Louise with the cleanup and carcass disposal, they walked back toward the office and front parking lot to Logan's car. Thanking her again for letting her come and observe, Logan asked if they were back to regular hours yet.

"Yes, we're opening everything back up Monday." Louise said. "I've got an interim vet lined up to handle emergencies. Hopefully we'll get someone permanent soon. Do you need to change your schedule?"

"No, I'm good," Logan said. "I'll be up in Portland the next day or so but I'll be back by then. Have the police said anything?"

"No," she said. "Not yet."

She looked like she had more on her mind but didn't say anything else.

"Okay, then," Logan said. "See you when I get back."

Louise was handling everything well, as she always did, but Logan could see she was as affected by Evka's death as she was, probably much more since she'd worked with her on a daily basis for over two years. Logan wanted to tell her about the Cormorant Coffee Crew, how she and Jean and Sam were working on finding out what happened, but she knew it was far too early for that. No sense bringing it up until they made sense of what they were finding and had more than just suspicions.

Instead, she spontaneously gave the stoic woman a hug, and before Louise could respond, got in her car. For now, the best thing she could do was get those phone records from Huey. Since she wasn't supposed to meet him until seven o'clock at

Thanh's restaurant, she stopped off at Jean's rental, changed, and went for a run. Remembering the paths that ran through the park behind Evka's house, she found a good, four-mile loop and ran until she broke a sweat. Then she went back to Jean's showered, packed an overnight bag and hit the road. She needed to get out of town.

KERNS NEIGHBORHOOD

PORTLAND, OR

Even with traffic, Logan was able to roll into Portland in plenty of time to meet Huey. Formerly a high-crime area, the Kerns neighborhood had become popular with hipsters in recent years. It retained enough of its shady background to be edgy, but not enough to scare potential customers away from the restaurants and stores popping up in recent years. Thanh's *Vietnam Pearl* anchored the block with a prime corner location, huge picture windows along both sides, with two separate entrances. One for the bar, one for the main restaurant.

Logan parked on the street and went inside. She'd been there when Thanh and her new husband, Faahim, first opened the restaurant a couple of years ago. Logan smiled at the memory of the first time she saw the handsome Syrian casting longing glances at Thanh from his food truck, *Damascus Dining*, which was right next door to *Thanh's Pho*. At the time, Thanh was a widow—her first husband had died of meningitis. Logan was glad to see her friend happy again. She had been through a lot.

Once her eyes adjusted from the bright light outside, she remembered how sophisticated, yet welcoming the new restaurant was. To her left, Faahim held court at the crowded bar, in the lounge area he designed and managed. In the main dining room, about twenty tables draped in pale peach, linen tablecloths were scattered across a wide-planked mahogany floor. White and black clad waitstaff flowed efficiently between customers and kitchen. In contrast, thick, reclaimed wood, open shelving lined the walls, displaying simple, elegant white dishware, all gleaming in the soft light. Fresh herbs spilling out of clay pots covered one wall from floor to ceiling, near one of the windows.

Huey waved her over to a table in the back. The only dish Logan was familiar with was *pho*, the traditional rice noodle soup, so she let Huey order from the extensive menu. Tuesday was a slow night, so Thanh would be able to come out and join them later.

When the waiter had retreated to the kitchen and they both had drinks in hand, Huey slid a flash drive across the table, which she slipped into her purse for safe keeping, then summarized what he'd found.

"I wasn't sure how far back you wanted me to go," he said, "so I looked at January and February, concentrating on the week before your friend's death."

"What did you find?" Logan asked.

34

"I'll get to the detail in a minute, but for the most part, your friend was pretty work-oriented. Other than her on again, off again relationship with Mia, which is well documented, not a social butterfly type. Most of her outgoing calls were to restaurants . . ."

Logan nodded. "I think I know what those are," she said. "Evka ate out a lot."

Next, Huey handed her a printout several pages long.

"Those are the texts and calls from Monday through Thursday night," he said. "The rest is all on the flash drive if you need more. Normally, you can only get these for a couple of days, but I copied and saved them for you."

"I'm not sure what I need," Logan said. "But this is a great start, Huey. I can't tell you how much I appreciate this."

"No problem," he said.

He pulled a gold mechanical pencil from his pocket and started using it as a pointer, explaining line by line what she was looking at. His hair combed neatly to the side, dressed in gray slacks and a blue dress shirt, Huey looked very much like an accountant, helping a client understand their taxes.

"The phone calls only have the number dialed or received and the length of time. No content unless they left a voicemail. I've highlighted those in yellow next to the names associated with that number. The texts we have in full."

So far it all made sense.

"So where do we start?" Logan asked.

"Well," Huey said, smiling. "I think you're going to want to take a look at both."

"Where do you want me to start?" Huey asked. "Phone calls or texts?"

"You pick," Logan said. Her skin was tingling. She felt like whatever was in Evka's phone held the secret to her death.

"Let's start with the phone calls," Huey said. He started putting check marks next to some of them. "I'll go through what looks like the boring stuff first. Other than the restaurants, there were several calls to and from—mostly from—these two numbers over the last week. One was from a local farm and the other from a poultry facility—some kind of chicken ranch," Huey said.

"Where was the farm?" Logan asked.

"Local, less than ten miles north of the center," Huey said. "Patterson family, small operation."

"Oh, that's where Evka releases rehabbed barn owls," Logan said. "She lets them know when she has some to bring out."

"What about the chicken place?" Huey asked.

"They get live chicks delivered for some of the raptors to eat," Logan said. "Circle that number, I'll call to make sure, but that's probably all that is. Setting up delivery times, verifying deliveries, that sort of thing."

Huey was taking his time, being thorough, but Logan was about to crawl out of her skin with impatience.

"Okay, next," he said. "These calls are all from Mia Schuster's cell phone. I underlined those—quite a few on Wednesday night, then a gap until one short call Thursday morning. After that, Mia called and left messages for Evka, but there aren't any return calls."

Huey paused to take a sip of his gin and tonic. "Indicating either that Mia didn't know Evka was dead, or she was covering her tracks in case the cops ever obtained these records."

Logan conceded that was possible, but reiterated her conviction that Mia was truly shocked and devastated by the news of her lover's death.

"There's one more I'll tell you about when I get to the texts, but the rest of these numbers, except these two," he underlined those, "look like usual business, matching the length and frequency of phone calls over the last month."

"Yes, I looked a little beyond just this last week," Huey said.

"Evka communicated with the director of the center, Louise Shimmel, and one short phone call from another coworker, Aaron Whitlock. There were several from her phone out, no call backs. Probably for takeout as you said."

"Is that it?" Logan asked. "No friends?"

"None that called or texted," Huey said. "Other than her relationship with Mia, Evka's whole life seemed to be work related."

Logan thought that was sad. She wasn't a social butterfly herself, but she'd always had one or two good female friends, deep relationships she valued to her core. She couldn't imagine navigating her life without her best friend back in Jasper, Bonnie, or her new Cormorant Coffee Crew cohorts, Sam and Jean.

"What about texts?" Logan asked.

"That's where it gets interesting," Huey said. "You said your friend's office was vandalized, right? Is that where the body was found?"

"No," Logan said. "We saw the office first. When we didn't see Evka there, we opened the next door down, ward 3. That's where we found her."

"Okay, well, I don't know what this means, but Evka received a threatening text that night," Huey said.

He had her full attention. "Who from?"

"Chrissie Virtanen," Huey said. "You know her?"

"Yeah, she's a student at the community college, works at the center part time," Logan said. Her mind raced to what she knew about the Chrissie, Aaron, Evka triangle. "What did it say?"

Huey read from another piece of paper.

this is all ur fault! You think ur all that UR NOT! Ur going to get what u deserve!

Logan sat back in her chair. "Wow. What time did she send it?"

"Friday morning 3:32 a.m.—that's just a few hours before you discovered the body."

35

Logan thought of the warning scrawled in red marker on the whiteboard in Evka's office. "Back off, bitch!" "ur going to get what u deserve!" sounded a lot more threatening. She could see a young, impulsive Chrissie throwing things around in Evka's office, but she had a hard time visualizing her killing Evka. And how would she have done it? There were no signs of violence. Trashing the office was a violent act. An impulsive act. If Evka had been killed, it was with skill and planning.

Just then, the waiter brought out an attractive appetizer tray whipped up special for them by Thanh. She explained the different offerings to Logan, pointing at each one: Crispy Spring rolls, Chao Tom or Sugar Cane Shrimp, and Cha Bo or Vietnamese Beef Rolls, and Banh it or Little Cakes, a green leaf wrapped around steamed rice in the shape of a pyramid, then smoothly exited to the kitchen.

They each took a sampling on small plates. Following Huey's lead, Logan dipped the delightful morsels into whatever sauce Huey chose from the assortment of small bowls on the table and dug in. Then they got back to the task at hand. Logan had no trouble listening and eating at the same time.

Between bites, Huey continued, "These last two numbers are the most interesting."

Logan's attention was dragged away from the food back to the printout. It was tough because the food was absolutely heavenly. She wished she could eat like this every day.

"This number belongs to someone from Evka's past, at least he was in her past," Huey said.

Logan's brow furrowed. Her mind raced through the options, "Her ex-husband?"

"Bingo," he said, "Mr. Timothy Bancroft."

Logan looked confused. "When I talked with Evka Wednesday night, she mentioned him. Said they divorced a while ago, before she even met Mia back in Kenya."

"Well, I don't know about that. I only know there were several phone calls back and forth from Australia to Oregon the week before," he said. "But it's the last one that looks important. Thursday afternoon. The same cell phone was used . . . but he didn't call from Australia this time . . . He placed the call from Portland."

Logan almost dropping her rice cake.

"Evka's ex-husband called her from Portland on the same day she died?"

"Well, you said she could have died early Friday morning, but essentially, yes," Huey said. "He called her the day before."

"He was *here*!" Logan said. "In *Oregon*!"

Here she'd been thinking it had to be someone from the center who knew Evka. Chrissie's text making her the prime suspect, but this threw a wrench into the whole thing. Her palms were suddenly sweaty, and her heart raced.

"Do you know where in Portland the call came from?" Logan asked. "How precise is the data?"

"Within meters. My guess is he was calling from the Hilton—downtown."

"Do we know when he got here? I mean, can you find the flight he was on?" Logan asked.

"I can check on that, but first, there's more," Huey said as the waiter brought out the main dishes. "He also sent a text. Sounds like a response to a phone conversation."

Logan was all ears. Maybe this would explain why he'd been in contact.

> *Tim:* No Evka just NO!
>
> *Evka:* It is 100% mine and u know it! It was part of my inheritance. Im not even asking for whats mine. I will give you half. just buy me out and we will be done. U have a new life let me have mine
>
> *Tim:* Not my problem
>
> *Evka:* I already talked with a lawyer, Tim. He says its mine. I have the papers to prove it. Do u really want to do this? Lawyers will cost us both a lot of money this way and you will lose!

"Well, that's clear as mud," Logan said. "Jewels? Rare coins? Art? What were they fighting over?"

Huey shrugged and ate the last spring roll.

From what Evka had said, Logan thought their split had been amicable, but something must have changed. Whatever Evka had agreed to in the divorce, she didn't seem to be agreeing to now. But why?

"Anything else?" she asked.

"Not really," Huey said. "Someone started to send a text, but it didn't go through. A Jimmy Townsend."

"The groundskeeper?" Logan asked, puzzled.

"If you say so," Huey said, putting the paperwork away in his messenger bag to make room for the myriad hot dishes the waiter was bringing out for their main meal.

"What did it say?" Logan asked.

"Nothing," Huey said. "Must have gotten cut off. Says he was driving south from Grande Ronde, near the casino. You know how spotty cell coverage is out there. Or he could have spotted a cop and not wanted to get a texting ticket."

"True," Logan said. "What time?"

"Around 10:00 or 10:30 p.m.," Huey said.

He folded the printout and slid it across the table to her while one server removed the now-empty appetizer tray and the other started placing a variety of dishes onto the middle of the table.

Logan remembered what Sam said about Jimmy gambling. Maybe he'd gotten a wild hair and decided to go try his luck on a weeknight and decided to stay over. But then, why wouldn't he have called Louise? He didn't report to Evka. Maybe a courtesy call since he usually opened up for everyone? But Evka probably had her own key. And why so late?

Logan normally didn't call anyone after nine o'clock unless they were really good friends, and it was important. Were Jimmy and Evka closer than anyone knew?

When all the food was on the table, Logan tucked the paperwork into her bag and picked up her chop sticks. Huey followed suit. Everything smelled delicious.

When she'd asked for Huey's help, she'd hoped for a glimmer of a lead, but Evka's phone records proved to be a treasure trove. Almost too much information.

From having no leads to follow, they now had two strong leads. First, Evka's ex-husband whom she hasn't been in regular communication with ever since leaving Africa suddenly starts calling, then actually shows up in Portland the day she dies or maybe before. No idea what was going on there, but they were fighting over something. His last call Thursday was mid-afternoon.

Then, Chrissie sends Evka a threatening text at 3:30 in the morning. She must have been the one who destroyed Evka's office, but had she killed her?

Dipping a crispy piece of fish into a delicate amber sauce, Logan took a big bite, and thoughtfully chewed.

Definitely time to reconvene the Cormorant Coffee Crew.

36

Thanh offered Logan their guest room for the night, but since the restaurant didn't close until eleven, the bar even later, she and her husband wouldn't get home for hours. Logan planned on heading back to Eugene after her morning run, so she decided to get a hotel for the night. That way she wouldn't disturb them when she got up.

Logan had a special fondness for Portland, but she had to admit the downtown area had changed a lot in the last few years. And not for the better. A few years ago, she didn't think twice about wandering anywhere and everywhere by herself. She'd walk to Chinatown from the Sentinel, to Mothers for a good meal, then spend a few hours at the modern art museum or Powell's—all on foot with no trouble except an occasional panhandler.

But tonight, driving through Old Town on the way to her hotel, she found herself automatically locking the car doors. The streets were poorly lit and flimsy tents sprouted randomly like blue mushrooms. The few people she did see out and about either looked like they were in a big hurry to get where they were going or had nowhere to go at all.

She remembered Sam saying one of the employees from the center had an investment property in Old Town. If so, it must have bars on the windows, Logan thought. She wondered what kind of investment it could be. She wouldn't start a business here and it certainly didn't lend itself to vacation rentals.

Normally, she would have tried to find some live music nearby, but even though her hotel was in a nominally safer and better lit area, she tucked herself in for the night and stayed there. The next morning, as the sky outside her hotel lightened from charcoal to dove gray, Logan crowbarred herself out of bed, pulled on sweats and running shoes, and twisted her hair into a messy braid secured with a rubber band. A light rain misted the window, so she added a jacket and headed out. The temperature hovered around forty-two degrees, but she knew she'd be sweating soon.

Thirty minutes later, hands on her hips, breathing heavy, she started looking around for a place to grab a quick breakfast. The rain had let up and bright sunbeams now knifed through the narrow space between a couple of buildings, lighting up the sidewalk. Gorgeous. She tied her jacket tighter around her waist and turned onto Third Ave.

Across the street, a pink storefront with a sign that read Voodoo Donuts made her mouth water. She jogged over and joined the line forming outside the door.

Unable to choose, Logan got the Voodoo Dozen in a box, including her favorite, the Bacon Maple Bar. If there were any left by the time she got back to Eugene, she would share with Sam.

Driving south on I-5 with Evka's phone records safely tucked into her bag, Logan's mind wandered over the events and revelations of the last couple of days. She kept going back to the sad tableau that greeted her Friday morning in ward 3. Evka's body on the floor, the open kennel, the dead red-tail hawk, the small table on the right with Evka's laptop, her half-empty coffee mug. That's what had been bothering her!

She made two calls, then reached for the pink box on the passenger seat before slapping her own wrist. She'd already had three, she needed to save the rest for the girls. Sam was at the house and Jean was on her way. They had a lot to talk about.

Donuts for lunch worked for Sam and Logan, but Jean brought her own supplies—a turkey breast sandwich and some kind of green slime she made herself. She poured herself a glass, then tipped the thermos their way and asked if they wanted any.

"It's really good," she told them, "You should try it. Romaine lettuce, spinach, lemon juice, some fresh mint, half an avocado and some stevia or monk fruit, whichever you happen to have on hand. You throw it all in a blender, and voila! An instant pick-me-up anytime of the day!"

As if to prove her point, she took a healthy slug of the stuff and licked her lips.

Logan almost gagged. There was no way in hell she was drinking that. She'd rather die a few years early than have to endure liquified lettuce and spinach. Ugh. And as for stevia or monk fruit, she didn't know what either of those were. The only sweetener she had on hand was good old sugar. She let Jean down gently.

"I'm good, but thanks anyway. And thanks for driving all the way out here on such short notice," she said.

"Not at all," Jean said, "Wednesdays are slated for ME duties anyway, so it wasn't hard to rearrange my afternoon schedule. Besides, I can't let you guys have *all* the fun. Seriously," she added, "I hope I can help."

Sam stuffed the last of a Purple Zombie in her mouth, licked her fingers and pulled her computer over. Logan played waitress and topped off everyone's mugs with fresh hot coffee then got the CCC confab started.

She handed the flash drive Huey gave her to Sam. "We'll get to Evka's phone records in a minute, but I want to run something by you first."

"Sure," Sam said, inserting the thumb drive into her USB port.

"It's about when you and I found Evka, Jean. I don't know if this means anything or not, but something was off in that room. Something didn't fit. I just feel like until we figure out what happened in there, we won't know if Evka was killed or not. We'll just be spinning our wheels."

Jean and Sam agreed. Logan started from the beginning, explaining her thinking.

"So Thursday night, Evka stayed late to help the hawk. Maybe his wound had torn open. It was impossible to tell from the necropsy whether his panicked flight around the room caused his injuries or not. The door was open, so she must have had him out of the hospital kennel, checking his wound or treating him. It's tough to handle a raptor on your own, but Evka was capable of doing it. I've seen her do it before.

"There wasn't much else in the room. The chart/clipboard, her laptop, and a half-filled mug of coffee on the table.

Logan paused.

"This is probably nothing, but this is what jumped out at me. That coffee mug was *Jimmy's*, not Evka's. His was the green one with the owl. She always gave him that mug to use when he came by. It was his favorite. Evka's was the plain, blue one and she always had that mug at her elbow. She guzzled coffee all day.

"So if Jimmy stopped by Thursday, that explains his mug being there, but what happened to Evka's? Why wasn't it there by her computer? Where was it?"

Blank looks from Sam and Jean.

37

Logan plowed ahead.

"When we found Evka, it looked like she had collapsed onto the floor dead—no signs of a physical attack, but what if someone put something in her coffee mug? If someone poisoned her, that would explain why the mug was missing. The killer wouldn't have left it there with traces of a drug in it for the police to find. He might have taken it with him or her, but if he was trying to make it look like natural causes, taking it would look suspicious. Right?

"And her mug *was* there, just not in ward 3. I remember seeing it upside down in her office, on a towel next to the sink. It stood out because most everything else on the desk and counter had been swept off onto the floor. It wasn't hanging up on the rack, so someone must have washed it out. And like I said, if Evka was pulling an all-nighter, she would have had it with her."

"I hate to burst your bubble, Logan," Jean said, "but unlike on tv, most poisons are usually not quick."

"Wouldn't she have put up a fight when she started feeling sick?" Sam said.

"And it's not easy to disguise their taste, even in coffee," said Jean. "They also often cause vomiting, defecation, bleeding, or foaming at the mouth and they'd certainly show up in a tox screen. Which it might. We'll have to wait for the results, but I'd be very surprised to see anything lethal show up, unless the killer is stupid and didn't realize traces of poison would make the police start asking questions."

Deflated, Logan sat back in her chair.

"Even if they used arsenic or some other plant-based poison that would not be commonly tested for, it can take over an hour for arsenic to kill someone, so no, in this scenario, those poisons wouldn't work."

"So," Logan said, "what we need is a miracle poison that acts almost instantly and can be administered without the victim knowing it, *and* won't show up when they test. Great."

Jean got a thoughtful look on her face.

"There is another possibility . . ." Jean said. "There is a drug that causes cardiac arrest and works quickly. It can take effect in as little as thirty seconds. I'd have to check, but I don't think it would leave any trace other than slightly elevated levels of potassium in the body. But that happens naturally, anyway, with a heart attack."

"What is it?" Logan asked.

"Potassium chloride," Jean said. "That would do it."

Sam was already googling it.

". . . potassium chloride . . . potassium chloride . . . here it is. 'Potassium chloride is used to maintain water balance in the blood . . . often used for electrolyte replacement and to restore potassium levels in a veterinary setting', but . . . ahhh . . . here it is . . . 'potassium chloride is the drug that causes death in an execution under current lethal injection protocols. Other drugs are used in tandem, but potassium chloride produces cardiac arrest in under one minute . . .'"

IN PLAIN SIGHT

"If they used the injectable form, there'd be no need to mix it with anything or get your victim to drink it," Jean said.

"But that brings us right back to how it got injected," said Sam. "Evka wouldn't just stand there and let it happen. She would know what the drug was and what it could do."

"Yeah, there are a few wrinkles in the theory, but we're getting closer. Potassium chloride would work," Jean said.

"Wouldn't the ME have found a needle mark during the autopsy?" Logan asked.

"Not necessarily. Not unless he was looking for one," Jean said. "Let me give Bart a call. We need to go over that body again."

When she explained what she was looking for, Bart agreed to meet Jean at the mortuary at 3:00 p.m. To his credit, he said if he missed something that significant, he'd want to know. He agreed not to bring in the detectives yet. When and if they found anything, he'd notify Tate right away.

While Jean went out to get something from her car, Logan called Louise. She asked if they kept potassium chloride on hand and was any of it missing?

Louise kept Logan on the phone as she walked back to check, but even before she unlocked the cabinet, she assured Logan that they not only were not missing any drugs, including potassium chloride, but never had come up short and never would. Very few people had access to the pharmaceuticals, she explained, and those who did kept a very close and detailed record of every use of every drug on the premises. There were precise protocols in place. She checked and double checked, then came back on the phone.

"All accounted for. Not a *drop* is missing," she said.

From her tone, Logan realized she'd obviously insulted the woman, but she had to ask.

Pushing her glasses back up on her nose, Sam said, "Well, that's a dead end, but the killer could have gotten the drug somewhere else. I did a story on the growing drug problem in Oregon last year. If you know the right people, you can get pretty much anything you want. They use burner phones. It's like placing an order on Amazon, but without a paper trail."

They didn't have any definitive answers yet, but Logan felt they were on the right track. Jean was going to check for needle marks. They'd wait for the tox screen and look for high levels of potassium. And even if the killer didn't get the drug there at the center, most anyone who worked there a while would know about potassium chloride.

It would have to be someone who knew how to administer it. At least broadly. Jean said the dosage wouldn't have to be exact, but they'd still have to make sure they had enough and know how much to inject to kill.

Which brought them back to another sticking point. Even if there was enough circumstantial evidence that Evka died of a lethal dose of potassium chloride, that still didn't explain how the killer got her to stand still long enough to inject it.

Jean came back inside carrying a flat, black, nylon bag with a handle.

"Have whiteboard will travel," she said, explaining that she kept a portable presentation kit in the car for the forensic classes she often gave for the college. She set it up on a table easel at the end of the table where they could all see it.

"I think best with a marker in my hand," she said, writing Evka's name across the top.

38

Logan started by handing Sam the flash drive and then pulled out the printout. As she went through Evka's phone records, Jean marked off three columns on the board under Evka's name, then labeled them. Motive. Means. Opportunity.

They started with Evka's ex-husband, Timothy Bancroft.

Motive. This was still unclear, but from the text and phone calls it was obvious they were fighting over something. And it had to be a pretty important something for him to fly all the way to Oregon from Australia. So they could check the opportunity box. Portland was only a couple hours drive away.

"His last call was from the Hilton hotel mid-afternoon. He could have driven down to Eugene," Sam said.

"And he's a vet, or at least he was. He would know about potassium chloride."

"Could he get that on a plane?" Logan asked. "I mean, do they check for things like that in people's luggage?"

"Don't know, but remember," Sam said. "If he knew where to go, he might be able to buy it here. I'll have to check and see if his license transfers, if he can buy it here legally or if there's a way to trace that."

"Do we know if he's still in town?" Jean asked.

"I'll check," Logan said.

She zipped Huey an email asking him to track down flight and rental car information. If Evka's ex was still here, she wanted to talk with him, see if he had an alibi and what he and Evka were fighting about.

"Should we add Jimmy?" Jean asked.

"I think we should add everyone she was in contact with that night," said Sam.

"Okay," Logan said, "Jimmy starts to text Evka around seven. No animosity between them at all as far as I've ever seen. And no romantic involvement. No love triangles. He's not an ex of hers. So don't see what the motive would be," Logan said.

"But we need to keep an open mind," Sam said. "He had means and opportunity. He's worked at the center forever, right? He's probably seen it all."

"Yeah, but that doesn't mean he'd know how to give a shot or what the drugs were for," Logan said.

"Wait!" Sam added, quickly pulling up another file on her laptop. Her eyes darted back and forth until she found what she was looking for.

"He sure would know," she said. "Jimmy served in Vietnam, remember? And guess what his job was?" She didn't wait for an answer. "Medic."

"I just can't see Jimmy as a killer. He has no motive. No reason to hurt Evka," she said.

"You're sure they weren't romantically involved?" Jean asked.

"No, they were just friends, and only work friends at that," Logan said. "But you're right, we need to consider all possibilities."

Jean glanced at her watch, then tapped on the white board next to Chrissie's name.

"Next up, Miss Chrissie V," she said. "She's the only one who directly threatened Evka, and she did it at three-thirty in the morning. What'd her text say, again?"

Logan read it for them.

this is all UR fault! You think ur all that UR NOT! Ur going to get what u deserve!

"That does sound pretty damning," Sam said. "She was pissed at her for something. Didn't you say she had a crush on Aaron?"

"Definitely," Logan said. "Moony eyes all the time. She wasn't very good at hiding it, either. I think everyone knew."

"And he didn't feel the same way?" asked Jean.

"Nope," Logan said. "He pretty much ignored Chrissie, but he hung on Evka's every word. He wasn't obvious about it, but I caught him staring at her when he thought no one was looking. I could feel the heat coming off him from across the room."

"How did Evka act around Aaron? Do you think Aaron and Evka were involved?" Jean asked. "I mean, they could have had a secret thing going on. If Chrissie knew about it, that could be a pretty strong motive."

"Jealousy's always a good motive," Sam said.

"Evka and Aaron worked well together, but I didn't see anything more than that," Logan said. "As far as Chrissie goes, I just don't know. She's kind of a loose cannon. I can't see her planning anything so meticulously, but like you said, we can't rule anybody out, yet. We need more information."

To save time, they divvied up their tasks.

Sam would continue digging into the personal backgrounds of everyone on their short list: Tim, Jimmy, and Chrissie. At the last minute, she added Mia back on. Even though they thought they knew what her calls back and forth with Evka were about, she had been in touch with Mia Thursday and had called several times Friday, although, of course, Evka could not return those calls. Mia either didn't know Evka was dead, or she was making those calls as part of her cover story.

While Logan was waiting for Huey to get back to her about Tim's flight, hotel, and car rental information, she called Louise to let her know she could come in to help tomorrow after all. She probably had the schedule covered by now, but hopefully she could fit her in.

She wanted to poke around, see if she could find out what was in the message Jimmy sent to Evka that didn't go through. She also wanted to know what Chrissie had to say for herself. If she could get the young woman to talk, maybe she would slip up or even admit to the threats and vandalism of Evka's office.

Aaron should be back at work now. If she got him alone, she could ask him what he thought of Chrissie, see if he realized she had a crush on him and if he thought Chrissie capable of violence-even murder.

And she wanted to help with the raptors. She missed being around them. Even the resident raptors. They were still wild animals and being near them made her feel calm. She also missed playing Bella. She hadn't picked up her violin in days and whenever that happened her whole system felt off.

Jean left for her meeting with Bart to re-examine Evka's body to see if they could find the small punctures that would indicate the injection of a drug.

The phone barely had time to ring when Louise picked up.

"Logan," she said, "I was just going to call you."

"Great minds think alike, then," Logan said.

"I know you said you were taking a few days off, but is there any chance you can come in tomorrow? Something happened and we are very short handed until the new vet comes on Monday."

"Sure," Logan said. "No problem. I'm back in town. What's going on?"

"Well, two people called in sick . . . and Chrissie doesn't work here anymore," Louise said.

Logan was pretty sure she knew why, but how did Louise know about it?

"Chrissie? Why? What happened?" Logan said.

In her usual direct style, Louise summarized the news succinctly. "The police talked with her, and she confessed to vandalizing Evka's office."

"Is she in jail?" Logan asked, wondering if Chrissie confessed to anything more.

"No," Louise said. "They asked me if I wanted to press charges, but after speaking with her and her parents, I decided not to go that route. Chrissie has agreed to pay for the damages and go to counseling. She made a mistake—a bad one—but I don't think having an arrest on her record will help her grow up. As long as she keeps her nose clean, I won't pursue that option, but I had to let her go. I can't keep someone that volatile and unpredictable around the raptors, let alone the other volunteers and the employees."

Logan couldn't argue with that. And as remote as it seemed, there was always the possibility Chrissie followed through on her threat.

39

The Cormorant Coffee Crew reconvened over dinner.

Her meeting with Bart ran late, so Jean skipped her usual salad and made do with Sam and Logan's delivery choice of the evening, which was Mexican again. They discussed their respective findings over a huge order of beef and shrimp fajitas with extra guacamole, then adjourned to the living room with Haagen Daz's mint chocolate chip, which Sam found in the freezer. It was a little frosty, but no one cared.

"Yes!" Logan said when Jean shared her news. "And there's no question, right? No way to explain those needle marks any other way?"

"Nope," Jean said, "It was clear as day once we knew what to look for."

She stuck her spoon straight up in her last scoop of ice cream so she could demonstrate. Spreading the ring and middle fingers apart on her left hand, she then pinched and lifted the web of skin in between.

"Right there—the needle just slips in, hidden in that little fold. Pretty smart, really," she said.

"So whoever did this knew what they were doing," Sam said.

"What now?" Logan asked.

"Bart was very excited," Jean said. "This gave him enough leverage to put a rush on the tox screen. They said he'd have the results hopefully in a few days."

"But you said potassium chloride doesn't leave a trace," Logan said. "So what is he looking for?"

"You're right, it doesn't, but if that's the drug the killer used, the report should show elevated levels of potassium," Jean said. "Of course, there's the remote possibility other drugs will show up in the tox report. She could have been a user."

"But there were no other needle marks, right?" Logan said.

"Just the one," said Jean. "And . . . . being thorough, there's no way to tell if it was self-injected or someone else did it."

Logan thought about this for a minute.

"We have to consider all possibilities," Jean said. "Evka could have been a former drug user who fell off the wagon. That would explain no recent needle marks."

"So if a large dose of heroin or something shows up, unless we find out Evka had a history of drug use, this makes the cause of death almost definitely a homicide, right?" Sam said.

"Probably," said Jean.

Neither Sam nor Jean was surprised at Logan's news that Chrissie had trashed her rival's office and warned her away from Aaron with "Back off, Bitch!" written in red on the whiteboard. It fit with the threatening text she sent Evka early Friday morning.

Unless other evidence connected her to the murder, though, Chrissie was only guilty of vandalism. They agreed that for now, they would keep her on the list, but keep looking.

While Jean got the whiteboard and did just that, something flashed into Logan's mind. Something that should have been obvious, but none of them had seen it.

"Here's a question for you—where was Evka while Chrissie was trashing her office?" she said.

IN PLAIN SIGHT

She looked back and forth from Jean to Sam, but neither had an immediate answer.

"I mean, Evka had to be there, right?" Logan said. "Why didn't she come running to see what was going on? Chrissie must have made a lot of noise banging around, throwing things on the floor. The animal hospital isn't that large a place. No matter where she was, she would have heard the commotion and come to her office to investigate."

Sam figured it out first. "Not if she was already dead."

"Yeah . . ." Logan said, quickly thinking through how that would have worked. "If Chrissie came in through the hall like we did, from the aviaries, there'd be no reason for her to go into any other rooms beyond Evka's office. So that means Evka must have already been dead before Chrissie got there."

"What was the time of death window?" Sam asked.

"My original estimate was between two and seven Friday morning, "Jean said.

"What time did Chrissie send her text?" Logan asked.

"Three-thirty-ish," Sam said.

Logan did a quick calculation in her head. "So Chrissie doesn't live that far away, she probably was at the center in Evka's office by four a.m., so that means Evka died before that."

"That helps narrow it down by a couple of hours, anyway," Jean said. "Whoever killed Evka did it between two and four. I'll let Bart know."

Logan felt energized. Finally, they were getting somewhere.

The two remaining names on their list, not including Mia, were Evka's ex-husband, Timothy Bancroft, and the groundskeeper, Jimmy. Logan hated to suspect the lanky, southern gentleman who opened doors for her and was such a big help to everyone at the center, including Evka. But they needed to follow the evidence, and as of right now, the evidence pointed to both men. There were still a lot of open questions.

Hopefully, tomorrow at the center, Logan would figure out how to get at least some of the answers. There was always the chance that whoever killed the vet wasn't even on their radar—some psycho targeting women at random—but in her gut, Logan knew it had to be someone intimately connected to Evka. Someone who loved or hated her very much.

THURSDAY, MARCH 3

The bathroom tile guy called and said he needed to reschedule, so Jean drove back to the coast, followed later in the day by Sam, whose editor was chomping at the bit for her to get back to work. A large shore pine had fallen across Highway 101 during the night, blocking traffic in and out of Newport and another tourist—angling for a better selfie—fell off the rocks in Depoe Bay harbor and had to be heliported out. Her editor said he needed her yesterday.

She could have put him off, but this incident fit in with a larger story she'd been working on about the cost of being rescued by air ambulance services and whether or not the patient should be liable for the exorbitant expense if they got themselves in trouble due to ignoring signs that said, "Stay Off the Rocks." She also wanted to include the risk that first responders, including the local Coast Guard personnel, took in performing these rescues. Was it just their job, or should people be held accountable for putting their lives at risk unnecessarily?

It was mid-afternoon when Sam's editor called. Logan had already left for her volunteer shift at the center, so Sam left a note and told her to call her when she got back. She had additional background information on Evka's ex and the groundskeeper.

40

It was almost lunchtime and so far, Logan's attempts at finding Evka's killer had been a bust. Hercules Poirot she was not. She wasn't even that woman on that show her dad used to watch, *Murder She Wrote*. Fictional sleuths made it look easy, but in the real world, people didn't confess to murder over tea. Or coffee, which is what she'd been guzzling all morning.

They had been so busy that all of the probing questions she'd mentally prepared remained unasked. Between cleaning kennels and aviaries and manning the rescue line, the only time Logan had even been able to sit down, let alone talk with anyone for more than two seconds, was when she, Neil, and Aaron prepped and delivered the food for the raptors first thing that morning. Mostly, they'd just made small talk.

Logan asked Neil about his camping trip and asked if he had any favorite spots. She and Ben were looking for places to go next year and she wanted recommendations. He said he usually went off grid, so couldn't give her much information about regular campgrounds. And if the weather ever turned bad, as it had when a storm blew in where he was camping in a remote area of Washington on this trip, there wasn't a friendly ranger or fellow campers to help you haul everything out yourself.

Aaron asked Logan about her music. He'd seen the infamous viral video on YouTube and asked if she ever played locally. She told him sometimes she joined up with Rheanna when she sang at clubs in Portland and promised to let him know next time that happened.

With only another hour left on her shift, Logan decided to make a last-minute check of the aviary enclosures to see if any leftovers from breakfast needed to be removed before she left. Raptors were messy eaters. When she got to Opa's aviary, she sat down on a nearby boulder to watch the beautiful owl.

A young, but fully grown female, Opa was two feet high, tip to tail and weighed in at almost twice as much as her male counterparts. That still made her only about three and a half pounds, due to her mostly hollow bones.

At two years old, Opa was just becoming sexually mature, attracting the attention of a wild great horned owl who lived nearby, as was evidenced by the plentiful streaks of white urea on and at the bottom of a tree that grew just outside her enclosure. Logan felt sorry for the poor male owl who patiently returned night after night to try to win her affections. Hopefully, he'd give up soon and find a more available girlfriend. It was a little late in the season to find a mate.

Great horned owls were successful in part because they were early breeders. They showed up in January, stole another raptor's nest if they could find one, found a mate and settled in. They had their first chicks when other raptors and birds were just arriving. According to Aaron, they arrived early because they needed the extra time to rear their young, who needed to be ready to fly out on their own in the fall.

Opa was a gorgeous creature. Sitting on one of her higher perches, she sat serenely in all her full feathered glory, blinking her large, yellow eyes. Logan had assumed those large eyes meant she had great vision. They did see better than we do at night, but she had learned Opa's sharpest sense was hearing. Her ears weren't visible, but Logan knew they were hidden on each side of her head, one slightly higher than the other to help her zero in on targets precisely.

She looked fairly harmless right now, but Logan had seen a video of a great horned owl in action. Poetry in motion. Rotating her head, pinpointing her prey, then gliding silently on fringed wings, never losing her focus, the owl reached out her legs at the last minute, stunning and capturing her prey in long, sharp talons.

Right now, Opa was relaxed, her feathers fluffed loosely over her feet and toes. She balanced perfectly on her branch with two toes in the front and one in the back. Being zygodactylic, she could also switch one of her toes from front to back. When attacking prey this configuration gave her more power. Opa's grip was as strong as a bald eagle's, and in the wild, she could lift prey almost twice as heavy as she was.

Logan spent a few more minutes just breathing, letting her mind clear as she sat and observed the owl. According to Louise, Opa might live as long as twenty to thirty more years. She hoped so. Opa would never be tame, but she was one of the few raptors who had been able to tolerate humans up to a point so that she could be an ambassador for her species. Logan hoped to know her for many years to come.

Logan was loving her new life. Time for music, for volunteering at the center, for running on the beach, spending time with her family. For Ben.

Speaking of Ben . . .

Logan looked at her phone. He should be on his way home soon. She'd give him a call when she got back. Before she left, she walked back to the office to touch base with Louise and see if she needed her next week. Before she arrived, she got a call from Huey. He had information on Timothy Bancroft's travel plans.

"First of all, he's using his own name, so he's not trying to hide the fact that he is here in the United States and not back in Australia. Once I got in, it was easy to track him down," Huey said.

"When did he get here?" Logan asked.

"He flew in Thursday, checked into the Hilton. He's still there but has a flight out tomorrow afternoon."

"What time?"

"Four thirty-five," Huey said.

It only took Logan a minute to make up her mind. Louise didn't need her until Monday, so she could drive up in the morning and try to catch Bancroft before he checked out of his hotel. Even if he wasn't hiding, she still wanted to talk with him. It was a loose end. He and Evka had been fighting over something and that something might be a motive for murder.

"Thanks, Huey," she said. "I owe you."

Tucking her phone back in her jacket, she went into the main building and saw that Louise's office was closed, but she'd posted the new schedule on the hanging clipboard on the outside of the door. She had Logan down for her usual Monday shift. She made a note and walked to her car.

She was hoping to bump into Jimmy on the way out, but he was nowhere in sight. She hadn't seen much of him all day. Hopefully, she'd get a chance to talk with him Monday.

41

Friday afternoon they caught a lucky break. That or Mercury was rising or in the seventh house or something. Tate didn't much care which. He was just happy he decided to check his email one more time before leaving the office. When he did, there they were. Jimmy's phone records.

Voss freshened up their coffees with the remainder of the burned sludge in the pot, then returned to their desks to go over the file together.

Townsend hadn't used his phone much, so it didn't take them long to go through everything. After eliminating work contacts, only one other number showed up frequently—and with a great deal of regularity.

Every Sunday afternoon for the last six months, Mr. Townsend made a call. Each call was placed around two o'clock to the same 615 number and lasted approximately ten minutes.

Before Tate asked him to, Voss tapped it into his laptop and looked it up. "615 . . . 615 . . ."

"Back east?" Tate asked. "South maybe? Who does he call?"

He vaguely remembered the director saying Jimmy was from the south originally. Maybe he called his mother every week.

Dutiful son. Tate's mother lived in Florida. He hadn't talked to her in a while. He'd have to give her a call this weekend.

"You're not going to believe this," Voss said, turning his screen around so Tate could see the site he'd found. "That's the number for Riverbend—maximum security prison down in Nashville."

He hadn't expected that.

Tate called the number, identified himself, and asked to speak with the warden. While he waited, he scanned the prison's web page. The warden's photo was front and center under the banner. Early-forties, buffed up, no neck, steely stare. Except for not having any tatts—at least none that showed— he looked like he might have been incarcerated himself at one time. Guess you had to be tougher than the inmates.

Six minutes and three transfers later, Tate was told the warden was unavailable, but would he like to speak with the Assistant Warden? He would.

A few seconds later, Assistant Warden Barbara Morgan came on the line. Tate put her on speaker so Voss could hear.

Morgan was very helpful. He apologized for only having the name on this end of the phone calls, Jimmy Townsend, but that was all she needed.

"We house seven hundred inmates here and over four hundred of them are high risk—we've got the meanest mother fuckers in the state," Morgan said.

If Tate was surprised at her lack of political correctness, he didn't let it show. He kind of liked her style. And the fact that it was past five on a Friday and she was still at her desk. A woman after his own heart.

"I make it a point to know those special four hundred really well. Only one's named Townsend. Emmet. Jimmy Townsend, his brother, calls every Sunday like clockwork. That must be your Jimmy. No one else here gets calls every week. They may start out staying in touch, but most family contacts drop off after a while. 'Specially with this crowd. Oh, and another thing—his brother sends $80 to the commissary for Emmet first of every month. That's definitely not the norm."

"What's he in for?"

"Originally? Arson," she said. "Set fire to a black church. Saturday morning choir practice. The preacher got all the kids out in time, so no one was hurt. They only gave him seven years in a state penitentiary.

"Inside, he joined an offshoot of the Aryan Brotherhood, the Pride. I'm sure you know this, but in any prison—state or federal—you sit with your gang in the hall. And if you aren't in a gang, you'd better join one quick. It's about the only way you survive. We don't know if Emmet joined up with the Pride because he wanted to, or for protection, but either way, it's blood in and blood out. No way around those rules."

"So how'd you get him?" Tate asked.

"Like I said, blood in, blood out. Three years in, he shanks another inmate. Probably his initiation. Says here they fought over table seating."

Morgan settled in to tell the full story.

"Apparently, the Pride's leader at that facility took issue when a 'greasy queer' tried to sit at his 'white-boys-only' table. The poor kid was new. Being both gay and Latino, he didn't stand a chance. The boss said something to Emmet, who got up and stabbed the kid right there in front of God, guards, and twenty eyewitnesses. Bled out before they could get him to the prison hospital. Emmet earned himself an upgrade here to our lovely Riverbend Resort."

"When does he get out?" Tate asked.

"Oh, Emmet's gonna be with us for a while." Voss could hear the sadness in the woman's voice. "Not too bright, our Emmet. When he does leave, I can almost guarantee it'll be on a stretcher or in a box. That boy doesn't have the brains God gave a bug."

Tate thanked Morgan for the information, disconnected, and turned to Voss.

"What do you think?"

"Let's see," Voss ticked off the list on his fingers. "One, we've got Townsend's truck at the scene; Two, we've got him there on the early edge of the time-of-death window; And three, he is in close contact with a violent, racist, brother in a maximum-security prison. I'll bet if we dig a little deeper, we'll find the Townsend family tree is full of rotten apples. Oh, and Townsend lied to us about some or all of that. I'd say that moves him up the list, don't you?"

Tate steepled his hands and thought about it. He agreed with everything Voss said. He hadn't gotten the killer vibe off Townsend when they talked, but sociopaths and psychopaths were excellent liars. That's how they got away with murder.

Making up his mind, he shut down his computer and grabbed his keys.

"I think it's at least time for another chat with Mr. Townsend," he said.

42

Foregoing her morning run, Logan took a quick shower, then pulled on her last clean pair of jeans and a sweatshirt. She would have to do laundry tomorrow. She wanted to get on the road so she didn't miss Timothy Bancroft. Who knew when he would check out of his hotel.

She caught her reflection in the mirror over the dresser. The emerald earrings Ben gave her caught the early light and sparked with green fire. Not only did they match the emerald on her engagement ring, but they were small enough to sleep in. One less thing to worry about. Ben knew his woman.

She popped half an English muffin into the toaster and put on some coffee. Her plan was to be on the road by eight, so she'd arrive in Portland in plenty of time to talk with Timothy Bancroft before he checked out of his hotel. Huey texted her this morning and reassured her Evka's ex was still there, but she needed to catch him before he caught his flight back to Australia this afternoon.

Carrying her breakfast to the table, she slathered the muffin with some peanut butter she found in the cupboard, took a big bite, then washed it down with scalding hot coffee. She thought about the questions she wanted to ask Bancroft while drying her hair with the towel she brought in from the bathroom.

She wasn't sure if Bancroft would even talk with her, but whether he did or not, she'd learn something just from his reactions to her questions. Her brother Rick had taught her that. Rick was a K-9 cop, not a detective, but it was a small department and he'd picked up some tips from the ones he worked with. He'd actually been encouraged to finish his degree and take the test, but he couldn't give up his K-9 partner, Charlie, his German shepherd. He loved what he did.

Logan was close. She could feel it. She tried to ignore the fact that she had no authority and no backup if Bancroft turned out to be dangerous and things went sideways. Logan had always been more of a do-it-now and worry-about-it-later woman.

Logan also firmly pushed into the back of her mind any thoughts of how much trouble she would be in if the police knew what she was doing, so she rationalized. She couldn't exactly pick up the phone and fill in Detective Tate—at least not without explaining how she had obtained her information without giving up Huey's involvement. It was only through his hacking skills that she knew where Bancroft was or that he had been in a texting fight with Evka the day she was killed. Nope, she'd just have to wing it.

She'd be careful. It's not like she was going up to Bancroft's room where he could kill her if he wanted to and leave a Do Not Disturb sign on the outside of the door before skipping the country. She was going to call him from the lobby, have him come down and meet her there. Maybe go to Starbucks. They'd be out in broad daylight, right out in public.

What could possibly go wrong?

10:45 a.m.

Hilton Hotel

Downtown Portland

After circling the block a few times, looking for a parking space, Logan gave up and valeted her car. She kept forgetting she could afford these little luxurious now. Having money in the bank from her music video took some getting used to. But she was getting the hang of it.

She trotted up the stairs and caught sight of her reflection in the glass doors. Her hair finished drying on the drive up and was now a mass of wild and wavy curls around her shoulders. She took off her sunglasses and pushed them onto the top of her head. That would hold her hair for a while, too.

There'd been a wreck on the I-5 and she was worried he'd already checked out, but the front desk clerk said he was still there. In order to get him to come to the lobby, she said she was a friend of Evka's. Which was true.

At first, he refused, telling her to tell Evka if she wanted to talk with him, she'd have to go through his attorney. Finally, she convinced him to come down by offering to buy him a cup of coffee or an early lunch. If he didn't like the conversation, he could just get up and leave.

When the elevator doors opened, she took stock of the man who emerged. Slight build, fair skin, thinning black hair, wire-rim glasses, mustard brown corduroy pants with a light blue, Oxford button down shirt. Shaved, showered, ready to hop on a plane. He looked slightly curious as he walked over, hands in his pockets. When he arrived in front of her, he kept them there.

They were the only two people in the lobby. He agreed to a quick cup of coffee but said he didn't have time for much more than that.

Logan hadn't thought much beyond getting there and sitting down with him. She decided to not lie exactly but infer that Evka had confided in her about their disagreement and asked her to act as a go-between.

"She just wants what's fair, Tim," Logan said. "It was hers to begin with. Her father would want her to have it."

She had no idea what *it* was, but she felt safe using the information she'd gleaned from his and Evka's texts. She hoped he didn't catch on that she had no idea what she was talking about.

"Look," he said, pouring cream into his coffee. "I don't know what Evka's told you, but that property was included in the divorce settlement. We each own half. Evka didn't want to live in Australia. She loved Africa and her animals more than she loved me. So I left. We had a friendly divorce," he said.

He lifted the mug to his lips and took a sip, "If there is such a thing."

Logan waited for him to elaborate.

He placed the mug back on the table.

"We had always planned on returning to Australia. We even had plans drawn up for a combination home and animal clinic on that land. We were going to start a practice together.

Needless to say, because of the divorce, only I moved back, but I stuck with it. I finished the house and the clinic. I can't just sell it and give her half—that's my practice, my life! I'm remarried now. There's no way I'm selling and starting all over again. No way! Evka's being entirely unreasonable!" he said. "That's why I flew out. I had some miles and used them. Thought if I could talk to her in person, she might see reason, but she won't see me, so I'm flying back today."

Logan decided to press the point. "But her attorney says that land is hers. It should never have been part of the divorce settlement. Her father gave that land to her before you two were married. Evka just wanted what's hers."

"What do you mean, 'wanted'?" Tim said. "Has she changed her mind?"

The dweeb was sharper than he looked.

Logan decided to hit him with the news and see how he took it. She could explain her lying later.

"Evka's dead, Tim," Logan said.

Tim's face blanched.

"What?" he said, his mug rattling against the table, almost spilling when he set it back down. "When? What happened?"

"Early last Friday morning," Logan said. "She collapsed at the center. They're still trying to determine the cause of death."

Tim stared at Logan in disbelief, "No wonder she didn't answer my calls."

43

Logan fielded Tim's questions and explained she worked with Evka and really was a friend of hers. She hadn't lied about that.

She really didn't have much more to add and luckily, he was more focused on her news than why she was there. She watched his reactions carefully, and although he seemed genuinely shocked by Evka's death, his main concerns were selfish.

"So do you know if she started legal proceedings yet?" he asked. "I mean, her parents are deceased, and we didn't have any children. Do you think the courts will give me full title, now? If you know the name of her attorney, maybe I can find out what to do next to get all this straightened out. Did she have a will? Since I'm the nearest thing she has to surviving family, I should be entitled to whatever she has, right?"

Logan was repelled by his attitude. She told him she had no idea and left him to pay the check.

What a piece of work.

She almost hoped he was the killer, just so he wouldn't be able to cash in.

She had never been through a divorce—Jack died before she found out about his multiple affairs—but she'd known enough people who had gone through one to realize that divorce was rarely simple or completely over, even after it was final according to the courts. Even if the couple didn't have children, issues like this often lingered. A teacher friend back in Jasper had given her house to her husband in their divorce, but when he foreclosed on it without telling her, she learned she was liable for the original loan. It ruined her credit for seven years. People were tethered together on many levels.

She counted herself very lucky that she and Ben found each other. He'd been burned and so had she, but somehow, they both managed to overcome past betrayals and love again. Ben was as solid as they came, and she never took him for granted.

From the contents of his texting argument with Evka and the greed and determination in his voice, Logan decided to keep Tim on their suspect list. He definitely stood to benefit the most from Evka's death. Now that she was gone, the lawsuit went away, and he got to keep it all. Unfair, but probably legal.

To wash away the morning spent with Evka's greedy ex, Logan decided to spend the afternoon visiting one of her favorite places in Portland, the Japanese Garden. If she left now, she could be there in fifteen minutes.

Immersing herself in nature never failed to calm and re-center her. Luckily, the garden was designed to showcase nature's beauty in all seasons, so she knew it would be open, even in February.

It proved to be just what the doctor ordered. From the moment Logan stepped under the *torii,* the graceful arch that marked the entrance to the garden and onto the winding stone path, the ugliness of all she was embroiled in since discovering Evka's body a week ago fell away. No murder, no greed, no anger, no hurt. Just nature. She'd process everything later, but for the next couple of hours, she would enjoy the luxury of clearing her mind.

IN PLAIN SIGHT

Places to sit and contemplate were scattered all along the paths, and Logan tried a different spot each time. Today she chose a small bench almost completely hidden from view behind a thick grouping of shrubs and Japanese maples. Ducking under some branches, she sat at the far end of the bench. Holding her hands loosely in her lap, she balanced her body over her sitting bones and took several deep, cleansing breaths. Her physical therapist was also a yoga instructor and had insisted she learn a few relaxation techniques after her accident to help with the healing. They worked.

To her right, a small stream burbled peacefully. On a large flat rock at the water's edge sat the largest bullfrog Logan had ever seen. She stayed perfectly still and watched it for quite a while. When it didn't move, she realized it must be a sculpture. It looked very realistic.

Time drifted and as usual whenever she settled her mind, pieces of music started floating by. Phrases, notes, sometimes whole compositions came to her in these sessions. She hummed a few into her phone so she wouldn't forget them when she got home, then got back to doing nothing.

Finally, the sky began to darken and the cold seeped in through her coat. Shaking herself and rubbing her arms to warm up, Logan stood to go. She heard a giant plop! nearby and when she looked at the rock, the frog was gone, and the surface of the water rippled away in concentric circles.

Well, I'll be damned.

Logan had considered stopping by the Vietnam Pearl to visit with Thanh, but decided instead to grab something quick, then drive straight through to Eugene. The new melody that came to her while she was sitting in the garden kept running through her mind and her fingers were itching to play.

It was full dark by the time she got through Salem. When she reached Albany, heavy rain pounded a staccato rhythm on the roof of her car and reduced her view of the taillights in front of her to two blurred, red circles. Rain in Oregon was not an unexpected event, but it was February and Logan was getting a wee bit tired of it. Of course, she reminded herself, that's why Oregon was so green. Beauty has its price.

She adjusted her headlights, turned on the wipers, and backed off the gas pedal to a safer speed. Traffic thinned. She was almost home. All good.

If she'd been paying closer attention, she'd have noticed the large, black truck that pulled in behind her about a half-mile back. They were the only two cars on the road.

44

Logan was mentally holding three phrases of music in her mind, trying to connect and weave the last two together when a bright glare of headlights appeared in her rearview mirror almost blinded her.

Some idiot was coming up on her tail. Some kind of truck or large SUV. For a second, the driver was silhouetted by a passing car's headlights. Tall, big, baseball cap, both hands on the wheel. She couldn't see the whole thing in the dark through the rain, but he was sitting high up. What was he doing?!

Not wanting to slam on her brakes in case he rear-ended her, Logan motioned for him to go around her, then moved as far to the right as she could without running into the ditch. She started looking for a turnoff or even a wide spot in the road where she could pull over and let the guy pass.

You'd better have a baby about to be born in that cab, buddy. What an idiot!

Her headlights spotlighted a solitary sedan as it flew by going the opposite direction, but other than that, they were the only two vehicles on the road. Everyone else had the sense to get in out of the rain.

Well, if this guy was hell bent on killing himself at ninety miles an hour, he was welcome to it, but Logan didn't plan on going along for the ride. She squinted into the downpour, making sure her windshield wipers were operating at maximum speed. They were, but she could still barely see a thing.

She looked harder for a place to pull off. She could make out a barbed wire fence running parallel to the road, on the other side of a ditch, but nothing much beyond that. Just an empty field as far as she could tell.

Finally, she spotted a break in the fence up ahead, a narrow dirt road on the right. She hoped to hell there wasn't a gate. She couldn't see one, but it was too dark and rainy to tell. If there was one and it was closed, this would be a very short trip.

She pressed a little harder on the brake, slowing down, easing off the road to make the sharp right turn. Out of habit, she even put on her blinker, although the guy was probably too drunk or high to notice. She couldn't think of any other reason for his reckless driving.

Her back wheels skidded, but she managed to make the turn in time. Her own headlights illuminated the road a few yards in front of her.

Thank God!

The wire gate was rolled and tied securely against the fence pole on the left.

Logan breathed a sigh of relief. She pulled in a few yards past through the gate and waited. She was off the road, safe. As soon as this idiot was far enough ahead, she could get back on the road.

No such luck.

Instead of hurtling past, the hulking, black vehicle turned in where she had and roared up right behind her. Bright, white light filled the car. Before she could register what was happening, the truck slammed into the back right side of her car with shocking force, flipping it effortlessly into the field like a Matchbox toy car. As she became airborne, Logan gripped the steering wheel and hoped her seat belt would hold. The car may have rolled again, but its trajectory was abruptly interrupted by a thick, dark oak.

As her car came to a rocking rest at the foot of the tree, Logan could hear the engine of the other vehicle idling, then the driver opens his door. She was too far away to tell if he was walking toward her or not. She didn't think he was coming to help.

Frantically, she tried to get out of her seatbelt, to get away, but her left arm wasn't working. Then she heard the door slam shut and the vehicle drive away. A huge wave of relief swept over her. She tried again to reach her seat belt to release it, but a sharp stab of pain in her arm made her think better of that idea. She'd try again in a minute.

Resting her head on the steering wheel, warm blood trickled down her face onto the dashboard, but as consciousness left her, she didn't feel a thing.

When Logan came to the next morning, her vision was blurry, and it took her a minute to locate her body in time and space. Nothing seemed to work well together. It's like there was some kind of break in the circuit between her brain and her arms and legs. Kind of a delayed reaction, or her body was just being obstinate, which wouldn't surprise her. That would just confirm what her father had always said, that she was stubborn at a cellular level.

She couldn't remember how she got here, but she was in a hospital. Unfortunately, this was all too familiar. She hated hospitals. Lifting her right arm, she gingerly assessed her injuries. The left side of her head felt a little breezy. For good reason. It had been shaved and there was a large, square gauze bandage above her ear. It hurt like hell when she pressed on it, so she decided to stop doing that.

She couldn't move her left arm at all. It was in some kind of a splint, immobilized against her body. It hurt to breathe or move, but she could wiggle her toes, so that was good.

Her vision was starting to clear, but she wondered how she was supposed to find the call button for the nurse. She couldn't move her head without triggering spasms of pain down her neck, so she'd just have to wait.

She was thirsty and wanted to pee, but only her eyes could move without hurting. She watched the old-fashioned schoolhouse clock on the wall an agonizing forty-two minutes before anyone came in. She'd expected a nurse, but it was a doctor. Dr. Patel was short, brisk, and irritatingly cheerful.

He told her she was both saved and trapped by her seat belt. It kept her from going through the windshield, but not from smashing her head into the side window when the airbag deployed, or from breaking her arm. He wasn't sure how long she had been there, but if a passing motorist hadn't seen her, it could have been much worse. Hypothermia at the very least.

Forty-nine-year-old Janine Currey, traveling home after having dinner with friends, spotted headlights at an odd angle in the field, kept a cool head and called 911. Twelve minutes later police and fire showed up, followed by an ambulance. Patel gleefully reported that the firemen had to use the jaws of life to open the top of Logan's car like a can of tuna and extract her before rushing her to the hospital.

It sounded like a very exciting story, but Logan couldn't remember anything after the moment of impact. That awful moment, though, was burned into her brain. Even now she could feel the moment of panic when the lights rushed up from behind, filling the interior of her car, and she knew for certain that the truck was going to slam into her and there was nothing she could do about it.

Dr. Patel summarized her injuries, in laymen's terms after Logan asked him to switch to from doctor speak to plain

English. "Broken arm—that will need a cast as soon as the swelling goes down—you can come back here or have your own doctor take care of that . . . miscellaneous abrasions, contusions, and quite a gash on your head. That one took a little repair work, I'm afraid you'll have to be careful in the shower for a while . . . sorry for the new haircut."

"I can always join a rock band," Logan said, getting a huge laugh out of the guy. Apparently, it didn't take much to entertain him.

Logan finally asked him what the bottom line was—when would she be stable enough to leave?

"Not today," he said. "I'd like to watch that head injury. Rest, take your pain meds, I'll be back later to see how you're doing."

45

A nurse came in and handed Logan the personal items they'd bagged when she was admitted. Logan thanked her and put all the essentials within reach. Water, cell phone, and the all-important call button for when she needed more pain meds or help going to the bathroom. After assisting her with her morning ablutions, the nurse hustled out to see to her next patient. Logan appreciated her efficiency. She'd have to do something nice for her guardian angel when she got out. Like teachers, nurses were the unsung heroes in our society.

She gave Ben a call so he didn't worry. She didn't tell him the full extent of what was going on, just told him she'd had some car trouble and broke her arm. No emergency, no need to rush down and rescue her (which was Ben's default mode). Once he saw her new punk look, she'd have to explain what really happened, but not until she'd had time to figure it out herself. Was this just an accident? A drunk driver who panicked—a hit and run—or had someone tried to kill her?

Teeth brushed, bladder empty, and pain medicine kicking in, Logan gratefully sank back into her pillow and closed her eyes. A few hours later, she heard someone scraping a chair across the floor. Logan opened her eyes. Tears welled up in her eyes. She couldn't help it. It was just so good to see that shiny black bob and those hot pink, rhinestone encrusted, cat-eye glasses sliding down Sam's nose.

"Wow," Sam said, taking a seat by the bed. "You look like hell!"

"Thanks," Logan said. "I stopped by Nordstrom on the way home for a makeover."

"How'd you know I was here?" Logan said.

"Jean," said Sam. "Ben called her to let her know where you were, so she wouldn't worry. He didn't completely buy your cover story, by the way. Jean didn't either, which is why she called me. I decided to come babysit until we can break you out of this joint."

Logan started to laugh, but quickly brought that urge under control. A sharp stab in her side took her breath away. She settled for a roll of her eyes and a grimace.

"As soon as you're released, Jean will drive out and meet us at the house. I know you'd rather go straight home, but it's closer and Jean said it's closer to major medical if you need it."

Logan reluctantly agreed, then got down to business. Things were happening fast, and she needed to bring Sam up to speed.

Sam pulled out her laptop. "Okay, spill," she said. "What happened?"

"I don't remember much," Logan said, "Bright lights, the impact, then I woke up here."

She described everything to Sam as best she could.

"Well," Sam said. "Sounds like I know more than you do. I called in a few favors on the way over here. Your car was hit from behind—back, right corner. High up, probably a truck or SUV—some kind of high-profile vehicle—popped you off a dirt road near mile marker 233 and into a field."

"From what they can tell, you rolled a couple of times before slamming into a tree," she said. "You don't remember any of that?"

"No," Logan said. "Who found me?"

"Not the driver—he didn't stick around," Sam said.

Logan felt a rising sense of dread. "Do they know why I was hit? Any leads on who did it?"

Sam looked up, "Best case? Guy was drunk or lost control of his vehicle. Didn't wait around to get arrested. Classic hit and run. But it doesn't make much sense a drunk driver would turn off the highway and follow you onto a dirt road."

"Worst case?"

"You know what the worst case is," Sam said. "Whatever digging you've been doing has hit too close to home and someone tried to kill you."

"If they were, why didn't they finish the job, make sure I was dead?" Logan said.

"Probably saw the headlights coming—that's a long, flat stretch in that section of highway—decided not to stick around."

Logan let that sink in.

"So," Sam said. "Let's start at the beginning. Tell me everything you did yesterday. Last I heard, you drove up to Portland to talk to Evka's ex about their texts—find out what they were arguing about the day she was killed."

Logan summarized her morning meeting with Tim Bancroft and her impressions that the man was small-minded and greedy but didn't give off the killer vibe.

"Didn't you say you looked up everyone's property and vehicle registrations? Who has a truck or a big SUV or a van?" Logan asked.

Sam pulled up and quickly scanned the appropriate Excel file. "There are three that would fit," she said. "Louise drives a dark green Ford Expedition, Jimmy Townsend's got a black Silverado, and Aaron's got a Jeep."

According to their notes, there was no record of a rental car for Tim. He must have taken a shuttle or an Uber in from the airport. Or the MAX.

"That doesn't mean he didn't rent one yesterday after you left." Sam said. "If you rattled his cage, that's a possibility."

Logan agreed and said she'd have Huey check. They talked a little more, then an officer came in to get a statement from Logan about the accident now that she was out of surgery and awake. She couldn't tell him much but promised to call if she remembered anything. He thanked her and left his card.

According to the coagulated gravy and meatloaf under the metal cover sitting beside her bed, Logan had slept through lunch, so Sam went and got them some food from the cafeteria. She returned with a fresh-off-the-griddle pork chop, mashed potatoes, green beans and two little vanilla pudding cups. Hospitals must own stock in some pudding company, Logan thought. Everything smelled great, but she could only manage a few spoonsful of mashed potato before she started to fade.

Sam said she'd get a hotel room nearby and come back in the morning, hopefully to check Logan out of the hospital. At least she wouldn't have to worry about getting her car back—it was completely totaled. Logan didn't look forward to the paperwork replacing it would involve. She was just grateful she hadn't been driving Lola, her prized sports car back in Jasper.

As the sky outside her window darkened, Logan closed her eyes and let herself drift. The night nurse, not as friendly as the first one, came and went. At some point, someone else came and filled her water jug on the table next to her. With all the beeping and rattling of carts and people talking in the hall outside, it was never completely quiet, but eventually, it blended into white noise.

While she lay there, she tried to reconstruct the events leading up to the horrible moment when she knew the truck was going to ram into her, hoping she'd remember something that would help catch whoever did this to her.

She had no trouble visualizing the earlier events of the day, her tete-a-tete with Tim, even visiting the Japanese Garden. A feeling of peace washed over her as she pictured herself sitting in that quiet place.

So calm. The burbling of the stream, the skittering of some small creature in the underbrush industrious mouse or squirrel. The bullfrog she thought was a garden sculpture the whole time she sat on the bench, suddenly plopping into the water.

Funny how that frog had been there all along . .

46

1:30 A.M.

SATURDAY, MARCH 5

EUGENE, OR

He let himself in, locked the front door quietly behind him, and then let loose, giving one of the kitchen chairs a savage kick, sending it flying across the room. He was shaking with rage.

How had things gotten so screwed up?

Getting a Diet Coke out of the refrigerator, he took several long drinks then showered and changed his clothes. Not bothering to turn on the lights, he brought his soda back into the small living room and sat on the scratchy, plaid couch. He needed to think.

Everything had gone so well. He'd executed every step of his plan perfectly. He'd gotten away with it! Evka was dead and his world had returned to normal. His job, his routines, were still intact. All he had to do now was continue living his quiet life. That's all he wanted.

But then in one lousy second, he'd let his guard down and BAM! If he didn't fix this, he knew he could lose it all.

It happened Thursday. He'd been back at work for several days. They were operating with a skeleton crew until they reopened Monday. As expected, the police hadn't found anything and finally released the animal hospital and took the crime scene tape down. Louise got a vet to fill in until they could hire someone.

Chrissie was gone. That stupid girl got herself fired, as she deserved.

He allowed himself a small smile. He'd almost forgotten about the dumb blonde, but it was kind of delicious to think of Chrissie angrily vandalizing Evka's office while the woman she thought of as her rival for Aaron's affections lay dead on the floor next door. He wondered if she even knew about Mia, or that Aaron had been a one-night stand.

Thinking the coast was clear, he had started to relax. He was helping with the raptor meals Thursday morning. Aaron had just left to deliver a rabbit haunch to the peregrine. He'd only talked with Logan for a few minutes, but that's all it took. He'd let his guard down. That's when it slipped out. She hadn't picked up on his mistake, but it was out there. She might remember it later. At least no one else was in the room at the time.

He tried not to panic. Maybe she hadn't heard, or not realize the discrepancy that negated his alibi. But if she did hear, he would have to shut her up before she remembered what he'd said. There was no way he was going to let anyone take his life away from him. For years, the center had been his whole life. He was comfortable here. He couldn't imagine surviving anywhere else—especially not prison. He could just leave, but where would he go? What would he do for work? He couldn't imagine working anywhere else.

He'd kept his cool and finished out the workday, then came home and went to bed, but he didn't sleep. Every muscle in his body tensed with panic at the very thought of his carefully constructed world coming apart. He'd already killed one woman whose betrayal threatened to destroy him. What was one more?

But how would he do it? He had enough potassium chloride for another injection, but no one would buy two heart attacks in otherwise healthy women in the same week or place. And he wasn't sure if he could slip a roofie into Logan's coffee. She looked too savvy for that, and he simply wouldn't have the opportunity like he did with Evka working late. No, he'd have to make this one look like an accident. A terrible, tragic accident.

Ideas began clicking into place. Yes, that would work . . . it would have to be soon. He knew Logan lived on the coast and drove back and forth to volunteer. She'd stayed to help out this week but had to go home sometime. It shouldn't be too hard to find out when she was leaving.

His opportunity came Friday afternoon. Louise had called to ask if he could man the rescue line that night. She said Logan would take it tomorrow. McKenna had spent the day up in Portland and was driving back to Eugene tonight, or she would have covered it both nights.

Well, one highway was as good as another. As long as Logan was on it and alone, his plan would work. Even better that it would be at night. All he had to do was pick his spot on the highway and wait. Logan drove a dime-a-dozen car, but she was kind of tall for a woman and her long, reddish hair would make her easy to spot, plus her Hyundai sported a large Cascades Raptor Center decal on the back.

There was an open stretch of rural highway between small towns where he could get the job done without being seen. She had to come this way. He'd wait until she passed him, then pull in after her and follow from a distance.

It had all gone like clockwork. The rain was an added blessing, helping to make him even more invisible, and the road more treacherous. When Logan realized he was on her tail, she pulled off the road, but she couldn't escape. Her car rolled and then crashed into the tree. Just as he was about to get out of his car to finish the job, if necessary, he saw headlights coming. They were still far away, but he couldn't risk being caught.

The truck was smashed in front and the hood crinkled up on the left side, but it was drivable.

If Logan had survived the crash, the only problem would be if she had seen him. It had been dark and raining hard, and he'd kept his ball cap low, but if she could identify him, it was all over. All his careful preparations and the perfect execution of his plan would come undone.

All because of one interfering woman, Logan McKenna.

He tapped his finger on the top of the empty soda can. He really needed to know if she was alive.

He looked up the number for the non-emergency highway patrol number on his computer. He pretended to be a concerned father worried about the safety of his daughter driving home from college. She came home from Portland every weekend. She hadn't arrived yet. She was never this late. Maybe she went to a party? She never drank, but . . . he was so worried about her. Had there been any accidents or fatalities?

The officer manning the line wouldn't tell him much, but he finally got her to let him know there had been one accident involving a female passenger who had been taken to OHSU. She was sorry, but she couldn't give him a name. His best bet was to call the hospital. He thanked her and hung up.

On his feet now, he threw the can away under the kitchen sink and spent the next few hours pacing and fuming. He couldn't call the hospital. He couldn't even call Louise to see if she knew how Logan was doing. He wasn't supposed to know she'd even been in an accident! No, he'd just have to wait. Fuck!

He hadn't been careful enough. No, he needed to eliminate Logan McKenna before she remembered—before she contacted the police and obliterated his world forever. Fury and hatred filled his being.

47

Sam was already there when Dr. Patel came into the room, looking bright-eyed and rested.

"How's our rock star this morning?" he said.

"Great!" Logan said, giving him a thumbs up with her good hand, trying to look well enough to go home.

She tried to smile, but since the bandage on her head prevented the left side of her face from coordinating with the right, she knew she probably looked more like a deranged poodle. Not the look she was going for.

Patel skimmed her chart. After bending down to probe this and that and flash a light in each of her eyes with his little pen thingamajig, he put it back in his pocket, straightened up, and folded his arms.

Folded arms were never a good sign.

"Well, you're out of immediate crisis, but I'm still concerned about that head injury," he said.

Logan glared at him, ready to fight. She wanted to go home! She *needed* to go home. She wanted to wash her face, brush her teeth, and figure out what to do with what was left of her hair. Her whole body felt like it had been tossed around in a rock tumbler. Every muscle hurt and if she tried to move her arm, she almost passed out. For fear he wouldn't let her leave, she didn't share this last piece of information with the good doctor.

"Let me finish," he said. "I said that is what I recommend. I'll sign you out, but only if you promise to see your own doctor within twenty-four hours."

That was going to be tough since Logan didn't have one.

Sam solved the impasse by smoothly stepping in, reminding Logan that of *course* she had a doctor, Dr. Jean Pullman, remember? The accident must have made her forget. Then Sam reassured Patel that she'd already called Logan's doctor, set up an appointment and would drive her there first thing in the morning.

Logan was impressed. Sam was a very good liar. All Logan had to do was nod. Which hurt, so she did it very slowly. Patel left and Sam helped Logan change into a pair of yoga pants and a sweatshirt she'd picked up in the giftshop. The yoga pants were purple, and the sweatshirt was emblazoned with a bright orange and yellow sequined sun across the front, but they would do for now.

Bundled into a wheelchair with a plastic bag full of prescriptions and after-care instructions in her lap, Logan waited at the exit for Sam to bring the car around. An orderly stood behind her holding onto the chair so it wouldn't roll into the loading and unloading zone. While she waited, she kept trying to fill in the blank spot in her memory from the impact to when she woke up in the hospital, but so far, she'd been unsuccessful.

IN PLAIN SIGHT

On the way home Sam drove through a McDonalds for an early lunch. This time, Logan was her usual ravenous self. She polished off a double cheeseburger and had started on the fries before they even got back on the highway. Sam took a little longer, but only because she was driving.

When they got to the house, the first thing Logan wanted was a shower. Sam got a thick, fluffy towel out of the closet and went to find some normal clothes for her to change into when she was done. While the water was heating up, Logan looked at herself in the mirror.

OMG.

The matted mop that hung down her back and stuck out on the right side of her head used to be soft, wavy hair. The doctor said she could wash it if she was careful around her stitches, but it was so tangled, she doubted she could even get a comb through it.

She stared a few minutes more, looking this way and that, then, before she could change her mind, she reached in and turned off the shower. Next, she hunted in the bathroom drawers for a pair of scissors. Calling Sam back in to help, she instructed her to grab a chunk of hair and hold it straight out from her head. Logan pointed to a spot four or five inches from her scalp.

"Are you sure?" Sam asked.

"Yep!" Logan said.

Sam obeyed and repeated the process until most of Logan's locks lay in the sink.

Logan ran her fingers through her now short curls with her right hand and critically eyed the results. Not bad! In fact, she kind of liked it. It curled nicely around her ears and made her green eyes pop.

"I like it!" Sam said.

Logan emerged from the shower ten minutes later feeling a thousand times better than she had this morning. There's something about *not* lying in a hospital bed being a victim, that helps you *not* be a victim. *(It made sense to her.)* Tightening the sling to secure her broken left arm more tightly against her body first, she managed to wriggle into the sweatshirt and jeans Sam left on the bed for her.

Now that she felt half human, she met Sam in the living room. Before she did anything else, she needed to call Louise. She'd missed several calls from her while she in the hospital.

"Logan," Louise said. "We heard what happened. How are you? The police told me where you were, but the hospital wouldn't tell us anything."

Logan gave her a modified summary of her injuries and said she was fine, but that she wouldn't be coming in Monday. She apologized for leaving them shorthanded. Louise reassured her they would be fine. Neil and Aaron were back, and the new vet was coming. Logan's only job for the next few weeks was to take care of herself and get well.

"So you can't remember what happened?" she said. "You have no idea who it was?"

"No," Logan said. "I'm afraid not. I don't remember anything after I got hit."

"Well, until the police track this guy down, do me a favor," she said. "Keep your doors locked and your phone nearby. It may not be related, and I don't want to scare you, but given everything that's happened and the fact that you've been asking questions, I don't think that hit and run was an accident. If you feel up to it, have your friend drive you home tomorrow. The farther away from here you can get, the better. For now, anyway."

Logan thanked Louise for her concern and said she would follow her advice. Sam was driving her back to Depoe Bay tomorrow. Louise offered to take her off the volunteer schedule indefinitely, but Logan nixed that idea. Yes, she was scared, but there was no way she was giving in to fear. She had a new life, now, a good one, better and truer to herself than ever, with Ben, her music, her grandson, her new home, and friends in Depoe Bay—and yes, volunteering at the Cascades Raptor Center. They were all part of her family, now. She wasn't going to give that up without a fight.

With that resolve, she and Sam decided to spend the rest of the evening talking over what they knew, what they didn't know, and what they needed to find out.

48

A cold front blew in and brought with it another three inches of rain. Rivulets of water ran down the dining room window. Sam tipped the delivery person and placed steaming orders of Pad Thai and Green Jungle Curry on the table. Logan breathed in the luscious, mouth-watering aromas. Just what the doctor ordered. If they ever had UberEATS on the coast, Logan was going to order takeout every night. A girl could get used to this.

They decided to share, so for the next few minutes, they focused on their food, then Sam pulled up Jean's whiteboard and propped it up at the end of the table. Logan wished Jean could be there, but she was still back home on the coast, working. Grabbing the last shrimp, Logan pointed at the first name on the list with her chopsticks.

Chrissie.

They agreed that although she was guilty of trashing Evka's office, she probably hadn't killed the vet. Besides, she didn't drive a truck and Louise said her parents were keeping the girl under pretty tight lock and key for a while, so it was doubtful she'd run Logan off the road Friday night.

Sam erased Chrissie's name.

"What about Bancroft?"

Logan thought about it, then ticked off the salient points, "He and Evka argued over property her father left her. She gave him half in their divorce settlement and was going to take him to court to get it back. If what her lawyer told her was correct, he stood to lose not just some remote property, but his home and his practice—at least the physical building. He definitely benefitted from her death."

"And he was here in Portland," Sam said. "He was a vet himself. He knew what drugs would be lethal and how to inject them. All he had to do was either bring it with him on the plane or buy it here. We still need to try to track that down—if he bought it here legally, anyway."

"So motive, means, and opportunity," Logan said. "But Huey didn't find anything about him renting a truck or car. He thought he must have Ubered or took a shuttle from the airport to his hotel in Portland. Besides, how could he have run me off the road Friday if he was flying back to Australia later that day? He would have been gone by the time I got hit."

"*If* he left . . ." Sam said. "And he could have rented a truck under another name after he met with you Friday morning. If you spooked him somehow."

Logan made a note to have Huey check on those two things. She tapped her chopsticks thoughtfully against her lips, then looked up at Sam.

"Okay, we'll leave him on," she said. "Next!"

"Aaron," Sam said. "He's got a Jeep. He was in town and has no alibi for Thursday night after Chrissie left his apartment and when he came to work Monday morning."

"He was home recuperating from his wisdom tooth extraction," Logan said.

"So he says," Sam pointed out.

"Yeah, but . . ."

"No buts," Sam said. "You said he was in love with—or at least had a crush on—Evka. She had put him firmly in the friend category, but he wanted more. Do we know if he knew about Mia? Maybe he was really angry about that. Knowing he had no chance . . . and speaking of Mia, why isn't she on this list?"

Logan didn't have a good answer for that. Mia didn't have an alibi either. She definitely had a temper and as a scientist who worked with animals, she almost certainly would know about potassium chloride and know how to use it. She hadn't thought to follow up on whether or not that drug or similar ones were kept at Hatfield where Mia was working. As for motive, maybe Mia was the kind of lover who wasn't going to let Evka go. And Mia was a large woman. That could have been her with a baseball cap in the truck that ran her off the road.

Motive, means, and opportunity? Check, check, and check. Sam added Mia's name where Chrissie's once was.

Logan felt discouraged. Their list was supposed to be getting shorter, not longer. She looked at the clock in the kitchen. Huey would be on his way back to the New School about now. She sent a text and asked him to give her a call when he got home. At least they could cross Tim off the list if he had kept his reservation and was over the Pacific Ocean when she was run off the road on Friday. That would just leave Mia, Aaron, and Jimmy. He was up next.

The phone rang just as she was laying it back down on the table. It was Louise.

"Logan," she said. "Have the police contacted you, yet?"

"No," Logan said. "Why?"

"They found the truck that hit you," she said.

Logan had a zillion questions. Why was Louise calling her? Why hadn't the police contacted her first? She put the phone on speaker so Sam could hear.

"That's *great* news! I knew it was a truck or an SUV—something big. Where'd they find it? How do they know it's the one that hit me? Whose is it?"

"Hold on," Louise said. "OHP found an abandoned black, Silverado, half-hidden behind some brush on the side of the highway, just outside of Eugene. It had damage to the front, left bumper, headlight, and hood. I'm sure the crime scene people are going over it now—they impounded it, but it looks like a fit for the location and amount of damage to your car, and the color is a match."

A black Silverado?

Something clicked into place in Logan's mind. She and Sam both looked at the whiteboard at the same time. To the one name they hadn't talked about yet. The one person Logan would never have suspected.

The next words out of Louise's mouth confirmed it.

"It was Jimmy's truck," she said. "They arrested him this morning. I was his one phone call."

Logan sat back in her chair, stunned.

"What did he say?" she asked. "I mean, are they sure he did it?"

She couldn't believe Jimmy would ever want to hurt her.

"He says he didn't, but he doesn't have an alibi. Normally, his poker buddies could verify he was with them all night, but this week, the game broke up early. He said he went home around eleven. It was dark, so he didn't notice if his truck was there or not. His parking space is on the other side of his trailer, behind a big bunch of wax myrtle. But the police don't believe him."

"Didn't he report it stolen the next day?" Logan asked.

"Nope," Louise said. "He says he woke up with the flu Saturday—sicker than a dog. Claims he didn't even know his truck was missing until this morning. Besides, if it was stolen, why would a random car thief run you off the road? What would be their motive? It stretches credulity, but even if it was a one-in-a-million fluke, why would they abandon it on the side of the road where it would quickly be found? A car thief would wait until he got into town. Find a big parking lot and switch out cars."

Logan couldn't argue with Louise's logic, but she still had a hard time imagining Jimmy as the man behind the wheel of that truck that tried to kill her. There must be another explanation.

"But why?" Logan asked. "Why would he want to come after me?

"That's the million-dollar question," Louise said. "We didn't have much time to talk, but before he asked for a lawyer and got his phone call, he said the detectives questioned him for over an hour. They seemed to think that he and Evka were more than friends and it was some kind of jealous thing, but I never saw that. They also knew you had been asking a lot of questions. Their view is that he perceived you as a threat."

Logan looked at Jimmy's name on the whiteboard. She felt sick.

"Anyway, I'm sure the police will be contacting you sooner or later," Louise said. She sounded very tired. "I can't believe it, but with all the physical evidence the police have against Jimmy, there doesn't seem to be any doubt," Louise said. "It was his truck, and no one can vouch for his whereabouts that night . . ."

Logan had no consoling words. Sometimes people were very adept at hiding their true natures. Louise said although she agreed to find an attorney for Jimmy, that was all she felt comfortable doing for now. They agreed to keep each other posted.

49

Before Logan and Sam could compare notes, the phone rang. It was Detective Tate.

The conversation was short. Although nothing was official until the investigation was complete, he wanted to reassure her that in cooperation with the OHP, they had located the vehicle used in the hit and run and had a suspect in custody.

Logan heard someone in the background and Tate asked her to hold. He must have been calling from a landline because the receiver thunked when he put it down on his desk. She waited for a few minutes, then someone else picked it up. It was Tate's partner, Detective Voss.

He and Tate might be tied up for a while, did she want him to call her back?

"Well, I just had one more question. Maybe you can help me. Is Jimmy is being held for more than the hit and run. Do you think he killed Evka?"

Voss was either less experienced or tired, because he was a lot more forthcoming than his taciturn partner. She heard his office chair squeak as he settled in to talk with her, his senior partner, now out of the room.

"In all probability, Mr. Townsend not only tried to kill you, but also murdered that woman. So yes, we have our guy."

She asked why they were so sure-what they thought Jimmy's motive was.

"You yourself told us he and the murder victim were friendly—he often stopped by for coffee with her. Work romances tend to be kept secret, of course. And I can't share them with you, now, but Mr. Townsend had a lot of secrets. For one thing, he has connections with violent criminals. I'll bet you didn't know that."

She did, but she couldn't tell him she knew Jimmy had family in prison. She assumed that's what he was referring to.

Voss must have realized he was saying too much, because he started using the words 'unofficial' and 'allegedly' and reminded her this was only a courtesy call so she didn't have to keep looking over her shoulder.

Logan thanked him, then heard Tate come back in the room. Voss handed him the phone. Logan wasn't sure how much he heard of what Voss had said, but before he could hang up, she asked him the same question, "How sure are you that Jimmy did this?"

Tate's voice took on a much more official tone.

"As I said, Ms. McKenna, the investigation is ongoing. There are no official results, and we will be very thorough . . . but, sometimes things are exactly what they seem. We'll look at all the evidence, but Occam's razor is well known for a reason— The simplest explanation is usually the correct one."

Before he ended the call, he added, "And Ms. McKenna, one more thing. I also called to insist on your cooperation from here on out and give you a piece of advice. Leave police work up to the police. I am very sorry about what happened to you, but if you hadn't stirred the pot by asking a lot of questions, this guy wouldn't have come after you. You need to stay away from this homicide investigation."

Logan didn't bother respond to this last bit but thanked him for contacting her and for letting her know a suspect was in custody. As much as she didn't want to think of Jimmy that way, she realized she was letting her emotions cloud her logic. If she looked at everything clearly, Tate was right. She just had to accept it.

Sam had only heard Logan's conversation with Louise, so Logan filled her in on what Voss had said and Tate had avoided saying. They rehashed the details, but in the end, but couldn't find any holes in the police's theories or the physical or circumstantial evidence.

Presumably, if they determined Evka had been injected with something to mimic a heart attack, they'd figure out how he obtained the drug and got her to sit still long enough to give it to her.

It was getting late. They planned on driving back to Depoe Bay first thing in the morning. Logan wanted to get home and Sam's boss had been patient, but she needed to get back to work.

"You need any help?" Sam asked.

"No, I'm just going to sleep in my sweatshirt," Logan said. "I can get the jeans off by myself. Thanks, though."

"'Kay," Sam said. "I'm going to hit the shower then turn in."

"Right behind you. I just want to sit for a bit," Logan said.

The rain gentled into a steady thrum on the roof. It was dark outside, but the edges of the woods were softly lit from the interior light in the dining room. She reached over and flipped off the switch. Gradually, her eyes adjusted to the dark. She could make out the fingertips of a lacy, western hemlock and a cedar, their slender branches peacefully nodding. She opened the window a crack to breathe in the fresh, rain-scented air.

With each breath she exhaled a little more of the tension she had held and allowed herself to feel the sadness when she thought of Jimmy and how they'd all been fooled by him.

She castigated herself for not realizing he had been somehow involved with Evka.

Evka told her about Aaron, why not about Jimmy? Maybe they hadn't been having an affair—maybe Jimmy was just fixated on Evka, and she didn't realize it until it was too late. Had he found out about Mia? Had that set him off?

And then he'd come after her. Her body tensed again as she remembered the terror she felt as she saw his head and shoulders silhouetted against the light, baseball cap pulled low. What had she said or done that made him think she suspected him? She tried hard to focus. She must have asked something, or he said something Thursday when they were all working together at the center.

She tried to remember any time they had interacted that day. They'd exchanged hellos when she came in. He'd been working nearby when she was cleaning out the aviaries, but they hadn't spoken then. Jimmy had been in and out of the meal prep area helping Aaron deliver the trays, but they hadn't had an actual conversation of any length.

She skimmed through the video of that morning in her mind. All they'd talked about was Neil's camping trip, Aaron's wisdom tooth extraction, and a little bit about her music. Nothing earth shattering.

There was something . . . skittering there on the edge of her consciousness . . . but no, it slipped away. Logan shook her head to clear her mind.

The irony was not lost on her that she was almost killed for something she couldn't remember or didn't know. On the other hand, if Jimmy hadn't come after her, he may never have been caught.

The whole thing just made her sad.

And hungry.

50

Logan shut the window, turned on the light, and went into the kitchen. A little protein snack before bed might help her sleep. There were some tortillas and salsa left from dinner and she found a half-carton of eggs in the fridge. Breakfast burritos! Even she could make those. All she had to do was scramble some eggs and warm up the tortillas.

The only frying pan she could find was cast iron. Ugh. She scrunched up her face in concentration. Her last attempt at using a cast iron skillet resulted in a stuck-on, burned mess. Ben almost had a heart attack when he saw her squirting dish soap on it and trying to scrub it clean. He informed her you NEVER used dish soap on cast iron. Which made no sense to her whatsoever, but she deferred to his expertise and had promised to learn how to use it so the food wouldn't stick in the first place.

Why couldn't Jean have cheap, non-stick cookware in her rental? But Jean was like Ben—quality all the way. Maybe everyone in Oregon knew how to use cast-iron except her.

Logan put her one good hand on her hip and stared at the pan. Okay. She could do this. She remembered she was supposed to heat it up first. Or was she supposed to put oil in the pan and THEN heat it up? How much oil? Was she supposed to use a special kind? Probably olive oil. Ben used olive oil for everything. But he also said it burned easily.

She got everything out and stared at the pan again. The shower had gone off. Time to bring in reinforcements.

"Sam!" Logan called. "Do you know how to use these things?"

"No need to shout, Logan," a male voice purred. "Sam's right here."

A chill ran up Logan's spine. She froze, then slowly turned around.

Neil was standing not five feet away, gripping Sam tight against his body with his left arm, holding a knife to her throat with his right hand.

"Hope you don't mind," Neil said. "I let myself in."

He looked a lot stronger than she remembered. She'd always thought of Neil as having a dad bod. She hadn't realized he was built like a tank. Sam looked like a terrified child in her pajamas, but she had a look of grim determination on her face.

Neil.

That's what had been bothering her. Neil was the one in the truck with the baseball cap. *Neil* was the one who slipped up when they were all talking, not Jimmy. She hadn't been suspicious of the dull man, the one who barely interacted with anyone. The one who was always there, but in the background.

He wasn't even on their suspect list, so she had only half listened to him when he told them about his camping trip. His told them about his tent getting ripped by a falling tree in the storm that blew in that night and how he'd had to pack up what was left of his tent and hike out in the rain. He'd mentioned the day, but the significance hadn't registered at the time.

"You said the storm hit Wednesday . . ." Logan said. "Which means . . ."

Which meant he came back from his camping trip two days early. In plenty of time to kill Evka. Which completely destroyed his alibi. She still didn't know why he killed her, but that hardly mattered now.

Quiet, boring Neil.

"Maybe you're not as smart as I thought," Neil said. "I assumed you'd figured that part out, already."

That's why he'd come after her.

"So you needed to shut me up," Logan said. "Why didn't you finish the job while you had the chance? Why didn't you just kill me then. Why did you leave after you ran me off the road? You couldn't be sure I was dead."

"Couldn't risk it. You were too far away," he said. "I couldn't have made it safely back to my car in time if someone had come along. And if they pulled in behind me, I would have been blocked in on that little dirt road. You really should have had the decency to die when you should have. You were a loose end then, and you're a loose end, now."

He adjusted his grip on Sam.

"And I can't leave loose ends," he said.

Logan's mind searched desperately for options. She could see Jean's knives at the end of the counter, but they were out of reach. With her left arm out of commission, she couldn't tackle him. Besides, she was afraid to move a muscle. Anything might set him off.

All she could see was his knife glinting right up against Sam's neck. It was the one he always had with him. She'd seen him use it at the center to open boxes or cut leather to repair jesses. It was extremely sharp.

51

She had to keep him talking. Maybe someone taking their dog out for a potty break would see the light and look in the dining room window. Maybe one of their phones would ring long enough to distract him so she could make a move—reach one of the kitchen knives, then scream bloody murder for help.

"You don't need to hurt Sam, Neil. She doesn't know anything," Logan said.

"She does now," Neil smiled. "I doubt she's going to forget this little rendezvous."

Logan had to try another tack.

"Why?" Logan asked. "Why Evka? What had she ever done to you?"

"Oh, that," he said. "She was a whore. Worse than a whore. A perverted whore. Not even a woman, anymore. But I took care of that," he said. "There was no reason for me to have to look at her, to work with her every day, knowing she was . . . corrupted, so I got rid of her. It was a clean kill. I took no pleasure in it. I just did what had to be done. You know how the raptors tear into a meal? Kind of like that. Just nature. I restored the balance of nature."

Neil paused, looking thoughtful, "I am sorry I had to kill the red tail. He was a beautiful animal. But he wouldn't stop flying into everything. I didn't want him to suffer."

But you had no trouble killing a human being!

"No one would ever have known. Until you came along. Babbling incessantly, wanting to know all about my camping trip."

Logan had to keep him talking. Maybe appeal to his vanity.

"But, how?" Logan asked. "How did you do it? We all thought she had died of a heart attack. When we found her, she was laying on the floor. There was no blood, no gunshot wound, no signs of a struggle. How did you do it?"

Neil's eyes showed some interest in her question.

"It was pretty ingenious, if I do say so myself," he bragged. "Potassium chloride. One shot and she was gone. That's all it took."

"But how did you get her to let you give her a shot?" Logan asked.

"Oh that," he said. "Roofie in her coffee. Simple. Evka never said no to coffee. When we were done, I washed the mug out and put it away. No trace. I of course took the syringe and other evidence with me."

He seemed so pleased with himself, he continued without Logan having to ask another question. "I tried her house first, you know. That's where I thought she'd be. I wouldn't have needed the roofie then. I would have just stuck her while she slept, and no one would have been the wiser. Heart attack in her sleep. It happens."

"When you found her at the center, didn't she wonder why you were there in the middle of the night, or why you were home from camping early?"

"Sure," he said. "I told her the truth. No reason not to. I told her about the storm toppling that tree, my tent getting ripped, by one of the branches when it fell, packing up, hiking out and driving back. The only lie I had to tell was about why I was there. I told her that since I was back early, I decided to come by to pick up any work that piled up this week, get caught up over the weekend so I could hit the ground running Monday morning. She was working on the red tail, and I offered to help."

Neil's eyes began to glitter as he shared the rest of his story.

"I was standing right next to her, looking right into her eyes. I was so close; I could hardly contain myself. In just seconds, I was going to wipe the world clean of her perversions. No more working with a woman day after day who had betrayed me.

Just as quickly as it had become animated, Neil's face closed again, shutting down all emotion.

"I don't know what I ever saw in her. She really was stupid. She bought it—the whole story—and then she *bought* it, get it?"

He barked an ugly laugh, tightened his grip on Sam, then looked at Logan with deadened eyes.

"By the way, I hate your hair. Women should always wear their hair long," he said.

As if taking beauty advice from Neil was high on her list of priorities tonight.

Then, Neil changed the subject.

"That's enough chitchat. You do like to talk, don't you? We need to get this over with. Take a seat," Neil said, cut his eyes toward the dining room, keeping the knife close against Sam's throat.

He was going to kill them. Sam first, then her. Logan had to take a chance. Acting on instinct, with her right hand, she grasped the only weapon within reach—the cast iron skillet—and spinning around like a discus thrower, she launched it at Neil's head with all her might.

Neil saw it coming and ducked, but not enough to completely avoid being hit. The heavy pan connected with a satisfying thunk, clipping him just above the right ear. He dropped like a rock. Sam scrambled out of his grip and sprinted into the back of the house.

Shaking, Logan stumbled around Neil's inert body, looking for her phone.

"Sam, are you okay?" she yelled.

It all happened so fast. Was Sam hurt? Logan had been so pumped with adrenaline that she hadn't seen whether Sam had been cut as Neil fell.

She wanted to check on Sam but needed to call 911 first. With her good hand, she found her bag in the living room and dug around until she found her phone. Propping it up on the couch arm, she swiped it open and started to tap.

9 - 1 -

Searing pain! Neil almost wrenched her left arm out of its socket, yanking her around until his face, twisted into indescribable rage, was just inches from hers.

"You bitch!"

He shoved Logan onto the floor. Climbing onto her back, he clamped his hands around her neck, and began choking her, his thick, iron fingers digging into her flesh.

This was it. She couldn't breathe, there was a buzzing sound in her ears. As her vision started to fade to black, a stab of pain jolted through her eyes. Then, nothing.

She hoped Sam got away.

52

Logan woke to someone kissing her forehead. She hoped it wasn't Dr. Patel.

She opened her eyes to see Ben's loving and concerned face.

"Hey there, beautiful," he said.

It took her a second to get her bearings, but she was grateful to see she was in her own bed back in Depoe Bay. Ben was sitting next to her, holding her hand. Then she remembered. She struggled to sit up.

"Where's Sam?" she asked. "Is she okay?"

Ben gently pushed her back down, careful to avoid her left shoulder, which was wrapped up like a mummy secured to her side.

"Sam's fine," he said. "And so are you, thanks to her calling 911. You need to take it easy. They gave you some pretty strong drugs. You slept around the clock."

Relief flooded Logan's body.

"Oh, good. He had a knife, I thought maybe he'd managed to cut her before he went down. I couldn't see her. I thought she might be bleeding out in the other room," she said.

"No, not a scratch on her," he said. "I promise."

"What about Neil?" Logan asked. "Is he . . . ?"

"Dead? No. In jail? Yes," Ben said. "From what Sam told me, it sounds like the police have all they need to convict him of murder and attempted murder. You and Sam will have to testify, but no one will ever have to worry about this guy again. He's going away for a very long time."

"But how? What happened?" Logan asked. "I don't remember anything after I passed out when he was choking me."

"You'll have to ask Sam for the full details, but she told me that when you launched the frying pan and clocked Neil, he released his grip, and she was able to get away. She ran into the bathroom, barricaded herself, and called 911. There was a patrol car nearby, so dispatch was able to get someone there very quickly. And it's a good thing, because you had already passed out by the time, they pulled him off you. A few more minutes and . . ."

Logan shuddered, remembering Neil's thick fingers around her neck, squeezing the life out of her.

Logan shuddered imagining what would have happened if he had.

"I don't know the exact timeline, but the ambulance arrived right behind the cops. They treated both of you at the scene, Sam said, but they took you to the hospital first."

"Poor Sam," Logan said. "She must have been so scared."

"Your friend's a tough cookie," Ben said. "She's already back at work today, writing up the story. Said she'd stop by later to see how you're doing. Oh, and Jean came by, but you were still out."

"What about Amy? I don't want her to worry," Logan said.

"Too late," Ben answered. "But she's fine. I'm keeping her posted and she knows you're okay now, just a little banged up."

Ben flipped his phone around so she could see the screen.

"Ian made you a get well card," he said, grinning. It showed a wild-haired Logan with half her head shaved, surrounded by a huge, red, crayon heart. Ian was too little to have drawn the image successfully. Amy must have sketched it from the description Ben had given her. He had signed it though. It was going up on the fridge for sure.

"The doctor said it will be a while before you use that arm. You've got torn ligaments as well as a broken bone. Nothing they can do for the ribs. Those will just take time."

After he made sure she was comfortable, Ben unpacked his bag and went to take a shower. He'd flown in as soon as Sam called him and stayed by Logan's side until he knew she was okay. Just hearing the normal sounds of Ben putzing around in the house made her feel safe.

It was over.

Thinking neither woman was going to live long enough to rat him out, Neil had told them just about everything. Questions answered, bad guy caught.

He'd even explained the one nagging detail that had bothered her before.

When Logan pictured the day all of this started, the moment she discovered Evka's body in ward 3. She saw it all very clearly. The open raptor kennel, Evka's body on the floor, her computer, and the coffee mug on the small table to the right.

But it wasn't Evka's coffee mug. It was Jimmy's. That's what hadn't fit. That's what had been bothering her about that scene. Evka drank coffee 24/7 and she always used the blue one. Neil had filled in the last puzzle piece when he said he had washed it and put it back in her office after using it to slip her a roofie. The roofie was how he drugged Evka to begin with, making her incapable of defending herself when he injected her with the potassium chloride that killed her a few minutes later.

Next, Logan's thoughts turned to Jimmy. His mug being there actually verified his story of stopping by earlier that night to visit with Evka and share the news of his winning big at the casino. She hoped he could forgive them forever thinking he was capable of murder.

Ben left to pick up pizza for dinner—normally, he would cook, but he hadn't had time to stock the refrigerator yet. Logan didn't mind at all. She loved Tidepool's classic combo.

53

LABOR DAY WEEKEND

Logan headed out the door into a dove-gray morning.

At the last minute, she added a light jacket. Summer was on its way out and fall was nipping at her heels. It looked like it was going to be a gorgeous weekend. As the sun popped over the horizon, white puffy clouds looked crisply appliquéd against a brilliant, blue sky and the sun sprinkled diamonds across the surface of the ocean. At Boiler Bay, Logan spotted a gray whale migrating south, down the coast toward Baja. She continued north to Fogarty Creek, then headed back to Depoe Bay.

Both her arm and ribs were healing nicely, but the enforced inactivity of the last few months meant it would take her a while to build back her stamina. That last mile kicked her butt.

She returned to the house around eight and was greeted by the enticing smell of bacon and the sight of Ben pulling cinnamon rolls out of the oven. It felt so good to have him home.

And this, they had decided, was going to be home. It had been easier than either of them expected to make the decision to move to Oregon full time and let go of their old lives in Jasper, California. Ben's nephew, Calvin, had not only taken over the landscape business, but gotten himself a girlfriend and was buying Ben's house as well.

Tilly had been managing Logan's math/music program, Fractals, very successfully. As Logan spent more and more time on her music and volunteering at the Cascades Raptor Center, she had been giving Tilly more and more responsibility. She was doing such a good job; it made sense to turn the reins over to her permanently. Logan would still consult with Fractals to supplement her music income, but for the most part, Tilly would be in charge. She'd introduced her to Rita and everyone at the New School and they'd hit it off right away.

Tilly had already been living in Logan's fixer upper and working out of the studio garage for a couple of years. When a separation from her husband became divorce proceedings, Tilly offered to purchase the property. Since she had few funds until her divorce was final, Logan was letting her lease with an option to buy.

Tilly made sure Logan knew she was always welcome to stay whenever she came down to visit Amy and her family, and of course, take Lola out for a spin. Logan would never sell her '58 Corvette convertible, a graduation gift from her father, but she doubted Lola would be happy stuck in a garage ten months out of the year in rainy Oregon. Tilly promised to take her out for long, top-down cruises down PCH and keep her in tip-top shape.

Tilly was also taking care of Dimebox, Logan's tortoiseshell tiny rescue kitten, king of his domain in Jasper, who now outweighed most small dogs. He and Tilly had bonded immediately. She spoiled him rotten and he was such a comfort to her, Logan decided to let him stay in California. Besides,

IN PLAIN SIGHT

Dimebox was an outdoor cat. Logan considered trying to retrain him to stay inside but didn't have the heart. And if she let him out to wander like he could back home, between the eagles, bobcats, and coyotes up here, he probably wouldn't last long.

So much had changed, and yet, the important things remained the same. Her family. Her friends. Her music. Logan felt it down to her bones. She was so lucky!

She came up behind Ben and gave him a squeeze.

Over breakfast they planned the rest of the weekend. As usual for holidays they were going to have a full house. Amy and family were flying up tonight. Ian wanted to see Opa, so they were doing that Saturday. Her sister, Olivia, a New York attorney, was wrapping up a case, but said she'd be here in time for kite flying and clamming on Sunday, and then Monday was the BBQ.

Logan checked her weather app. *Awesome!* It looked like the sun was going to stick around through the middle of next week.

Sam and Tim were bringing fresh crab and Chinook salmon. Jean and her husband were supplying the wine and a gourmet charcuterie board. Ben was doing his usual ribs, corn on the cob, and always a bratwurst in memory of Purgatory, his Greater Swiss Mountain dog who'd passed away last year. Brats were Purgatory's favorite snack and the cause of his legendary, lethal sausage farts. Their handyman and friend, Clay, and his wife said they'd bring a big tossed salad. Logan's contribution was picking up some marionberry and apple pies from Chalet in Newport and plenty of ice cream.

After Ben left with his list for the grocery store, Sam stopped by to help Logan string some garden lights around the deck. It had been a month since they both testified at Neil's murder trial and Logan, for one, was glad that terror was beginning to fade. The prosecution brought their A game and to everyone but Neil's satisfaction, he had received the death penalty. Oregon hadn't executed anyone since 1962, and no one could bring Evka back, but at least he was locked away for the rest of his life and would never be able to harm anyone else.

When they were satisfied with the lights and tested them to make sure they all worked, Sam went into the kitchen and brought back two, cold mineral waters. She lowered herself onto the chair next to Logan, both facing toward the ocean to take in the view.

Lowering did not come as easily as it had a few months ago. She had to undo the top button on her jeans. Sam was only four months pregnant, but because of her tiny stature, was already in need of maternity clothes. This also explained her choice of beverage. Normally, Sam was a beer girl.

Logan had news to share. "Remember Jimmy?" she asked, referring to Jimmy Townsend, the groundskeeper at the Cascades Raptor Center.

"Sure," Sam said. "What about him? I know he took some time off. Did he ever come back to work?"

"No," Logan said. "Louise asked him to stay, but he said he wanted to take some time off first before deciding what to do."

Sam nodded, "Makes sense."

"Jimmy won a chunk of money at Spirit Mountain. He was going to loan it to Evka to help her and Louise improve and extend the raptor center. Presumably, she would add it to the money she hoped to get by selling her property in Australia— once her attorney got her divorce settlement straightened out."

"Oh, yeah. Whatever happened to that? Does Bancroft get to keep it?" Sam asked.

"As far as I know," Logan said. "He flew back to Australia. Evka had no children or surviving family, so I guess things will stay as they are."

"What about Jimmy?"

"Turns out he has a brother in prison in Tennessee. Louise said Jimmy spent some of his winnings to get his brother psychologically evaluated. He may be able to get him moved to a private psychiatric hospital because the doctor says he is incompetent and should never have been made to stand trial in the first place. *And* he had a wet-behind-the-ears public defender for a lawyer. He became violent in the system, and he'll never be able to be free, but it looks like maybe he will be able to spend the rest of his years in a safer place. Jimmy's moving back there to be near him so he can visit him in person."

Before Sam could ask, Logan added, "And he says he holds no grudge against Louise or anyone for thinking he was capable of killing Evka. All the evidence pointed to him and from his time in Vietnam, he says he knows any of us is capable of taking a life, given the right—or wrong—circumstances."

Sobering thought.

54

Sunlight dappled the parking lot through the trees. They'd arrived before the center opened to the public, so they had their choice of spaces. Logan pulled into her usual spot. Before the engine was even off, Ian had unbuckled his seatbelt, scrambling to get out of the car. The five-year-old was beyond excited about getting to see so many raptors in one place, including Opa, the great horned owl he'd fallen in love with when Aaron brought her out to the Orange Coast Aquarium in Newport as part of the center's ambassador program.

Aaron didn't normally work Saturdays, but he'd agreed to come in and put Opa through her paces for Logan's grandson.

Louise came out to meet them and gave Ian a bundle of treasures from the gift shop, including a t-shirt, a mug, and an owl coloring book. Amy thanked her and helped Ian into his new t-shirt, which he insisted on wearing right away. Lethe,

the turkey vulture, wandered by on the path just then, and they all enjoyed Ian's shocked reaction when they told him about his unique bathroom habits.

Then, with a twinkle in her eye, Louise asked Ian if he wanted to see something his Grandma Logan had been working on. Ian, of course, jumped up and down and said yes.

"Okay, but you'll have to promise to be very quiet," Louise said. "Do you think you can do that, Ian?"

Ian clamped his mouth shut and nodded emphatically, his eyes wide.

Louise took Ian's hand and led them all back to an aviary away from the public area. She found a place for Ian and Amy to sit and observe while Logan buckled on a belt with a variety of pouches and tools hanging off it. She loaded one of the pouches with bits of fresh meat and pulled on a thick, leather glove. She smiled at Ian and let herself into the enclosure. Inside, up in the corner of the enclosure, a small great horned owl sat on a plywood platform, eyeing them all.

Louise narrated in a low, quiet voice, "This is Cairo. As you can see, he is a great horned owl like Opa, but probably about a year younger. Your grandmother has been working with him for a couple of months now."

Logan reached into one of the pouches and tossed a scrap of meat onto a lower platform about five feet away from where the young owl sat. He bobbed his head, ruffled his feathers, then swooped down to eat it. She repeated this action a few times. The last target was a simple scale with a sturdy wooden dowel on top, wrapped in Astro turf. The owl hesitated, then flew to where he was supposed to go to get his food.

"That's how we get them to weigh themselves. It's one of the ways we know if they are healthy or not," Louise whispered to Ian. "Now, this might not work, but there's a behavior your grandmother has been working on with Cairo that is very important. It will tell her whether Cairo trusts her or not.

She'd going to ask him to fly to her glove. We call that 'glove up'. If he can do that, that's a huge step!"

Ian watched intently as Logan reached into the pouch again and selected another piece of meat. She made a loose fist, tucked the piece of food in, then and extended her arm slightly away from her body.

Everyone held their breath. Cairo ruffled his feathers and preened a bit, casting glances at Logan occasionally. He eyed his perch back up in the corner.

Then he spread his wings and flew directly to Logan. Landing confidently on her glove, he dug his beak into her fist and snatched up the meat. In a few gulps, he got it down his throat whole, then blinked his big, yellow eyes as if to say, "What? I do this all the time."

✷✷✷✷✷

Worn out by all the excitement, Ian fell asleep in the car on the way home. That night, Clay and his wife, Belinda, came over to babysit so the adults could go out for dinner. Their grandchildren lived back east, and they rarely got to see them, so they always insisted on getting at least one night with Ian when he and his family came to visit.

No one felt like dressing up, so they decided to go to the Black Squid, a beerhouse twenty minutes north that had nineteen rotating taps of fresh beer, mead, and cider. Rough-hewn picnic tables lined one wall and there were a couple of dart boards in the back. Dog friendly and bring-you-own-food if you want to, it was one of those unique, Northwesty places Logan loved. Too lazy to cook, they opted for the taco truck parked under an overhang in front, dashing back inside while juggling their piping hot dinners just in time for the trivia night to begin.

Each trivia night featured a different theme. Tonight, the categories all had to do with flora and fauna of the Pacific Northwest. A young couple, the owners of the Black Squid, took turns running the show. This week's game show host was the husband, a thirty-something bearded man named Oscar. He was funny and kept up the pace, making sure everyone took breaks for more beer. Ben was their designated driver, so the other three were free to indulge. They decided to call themselves the Algae Blooms.

An hour and a half later, the Seastars, a group of tourists from Lincoln City, and the Algae Blooms were tied. It was the last question of the night. Oscar pulled a question out of the bowl, read it silently to himself, then stroked his beard and yelled back at his wife, "No one's going to get this one, Sally!" Sally pulled another beer and shrugged with a grin. "Life's tough in the fast lane!"

"Okay," he said, "here we go!"

He reminded everyone not to shout the answer out, as that would be an automatic disqualification, as one team had discovered earlier, then read from the paper.

Most raptors defecate by shooting their urea *away* from their bodies . . ."

"Often with direct hits, as anyone who lives on the coast knows!" a patron shouted out.

Everyone laughed.

Oscar held up his hand for quiet and finished reading the question.

". . . But not *this* raptor. This raptor defecates straight down his legs. What is the name of this well-known PNW raptor?"

Immediately, Amy and Logan looked at each other and high-fived! Ben and Liam just looked blank. Logan leaned over and whispered to Ben, 'Don't worry, we got this!' while Amy scribbled the answer on a piece of paper and turned it in.

Oscar quickly went through the slips of paper, then said, "Well, I'll be damned. One group got it right! Algae Blooms, what is the PNW raptor that pees and poops straight down its legs?"

Logan and Amy shouted out the answer simultaneously, "Turkey Vulture!"

"Come on up here, Algae Blooms! You win!" Oscar announced.

They divvied up their prizes when they got home. Beer mugs for Clay and Belinda, a glass float for Amy and Liam to take back to California, and a crocheted squid for Ian when he woke up the next morning. Everyone said their good nights. Ben and Logan pulled on their warm jackets and Black Squid beanies and went out onto the deck for a nightcap before turning in. They settled into their chairs and looked out over the ocean.

Ben put his arm around Logan's shoulders and pulled her close. Neither felt the need to talk. Logan's heart was so full, she couldn't have spoken without blubbering, anyway. She blinked to clear the tears from her eyes. Gratitude for all she had welled up within her.

As they settled into the quiet, the night sounds began to make themselves known: The ocean's susurrations, the rustling of the trees, the skittering of mice, and punctuating the base line now and then, the long low hoot of a great horned owl.

The threads of a new composition began forming in Logan's mind. She'd have to get Bella out tomorrow.

ACKNOWLEDGMENTS

Wow. I can't believe it's been almost ten years since Logan first began taking shape in my mind. I'm still enjoying seeing where she'll take me next.

And it's always someplace new. Logan has wandered in and out of the worlds of glassblowing, sea otters, rare coins, mineral rights, powwows, commercial fishing, Vietnamese culture, violin making, Appalachian dialect, coal mining, immigration, chess, Portland, Oregon, the ocean, music/math connections, obsidian, probate law, abused women's underground railroads, rum running, mental hospitals, and K-9 dog training.

With this array of topics, I need a lot of help, so I turn to the experts. I leave my interview questions wide open, and often some bit of information they share with me suggests a plot point which turns the story in a whole new direction. I love it when that happens!

In Plain Sight features raptors. Since moving to Oregon full time a few years ago, I have been fascinated by them. In the forest behind us, in the nearby cove, and during walks along the rocky bluffs, I regularly see bald eagles, owls, hawks, ospreys, and many other birds, so I knew I wanted this book to feature raptors, somehow.

That's where the Cascades Raptor Center in Eugene, OR came in. Louise Shimmel, the founder—and at that time, the director of the center—invited me to come out one day for a visit. She set me up with the bird curator, Kit Lacy, who gave me a great tour and patiently answered my questions, then Deputy Director, Julie Collins, brought me back to Louise's office where she generously spent another two hours helping me understand how it all worked and sharing stories of her early days with raptors. I wish more of those stories could have made it into the book. Karen Hall, who worked briefly with the resident raptors at the center before joining the admin team, also answered my questions and provided insights – she would visit the birds each day on her way out.

Over the following months, as I wrote the story, Louise retired from her position, but generously continued to answer my questions as they came up via email. Wonderful woman. You can read more about her and the center itself at Cascades-RaptorCenter.org.

Oh, and Kit was the one who told me about Lethe, the turkey vulture. He is a real raptor and yes, they really do poop and pee down their legs. Such a great detail to include in the story. Thanks, Kit!

Technical questions regarding dead bodies are answered intelligently and with good humor by Marilyn Fraser, Lincoln City physician and real live medical examiner here in Lincoln County.

People always ask how a story makes it from the inkling of an idea to an actual book. There are many steps, but here's a quick rundown of the process. When I've written the first draft, I let it sit for a while, then go back and tinker with it. When it is in pretty good shape, I send it off to my Beta Readers.

Beta Readers are the unsung heroes of every author's world. They are also a well-guarded secret, so I won't mention them by name, but they are invaluable in helping me find errors, rough spots, or problems I would otherwise miss. So a huge thank you to all of you, you know who you are!

Next, I begin work with my editor, interior designer, and cover designer, Kimberly Peticolas, who always does a stellar job, taking the book from start to finish with elegant style. Any remaining errors are all mine.

Finally, I'd like to thank my faithful readers. Every one of you who pre-orders or purchases my books online, buys them in stores, or directly from me at book fairs is valued. And I'd like to thank you twice if you also take the time to leave a review on Amazon, BookBub, Goodreads, or other sites. As an independent author, it means a lot to me.

Another fun thing I look forward to with each book is the Character Naming Contest. For *In Plain Sight*, congratulations to Meredith Leonard, who selected 'Opa' as the name for the two-year-old great horned owl featured on the front cover.

The bulk of my thanks is reserved for my husband, John, who puts up with having an MIA wife for months at a time while I birth books. I can't imagine listening to the rain on the skylights while playing our evening game of chess or cards in front of the fire with anyone else.

ABOUT THE AUTHOR

A self-admitted book addict, Valerie Davisson was the kid with the flashlight under her pillow, reading long after lights out. After a life of travel, she now lives on the Oregon coast with her husband, John, and their new puppy, Finn. When not working on her latest book, she's probably in the kitchen, cooking up a storm for family and friends.

Enjoyed the Book?

If you enjoyed *In Plain Sight*, please consider leaving a review on Amazon or Goodreads. And be sure to check out the rest of the Logan McKenna series.

Shattered (Book 1)
Forest Park (Book 2)
Devil's Claw (Book 3)
Vanishing Day (Book 4)
Safe Harbor (Book 5)
Lies That Bind (Book 6)
Whisper Creek (Book 7)

Want to know more about Valerie Davisson or her next book? Make sure to visit valeriedavisson.com and sign up for her newsletter.

CASCADES RAPTOR CENTER

WHY DO THESE RAPTORS NEED OUR HELP?

The vast majority have been the losers in some confrontation with humans or our way of life: these birds are in collisions with vehicles; hit windows or come down chimneys; hit power lines; tangle in fishing line, or barbed wire, electric, or other fencing; are poisoned by rodenticides or pesticides; are shot; are caught in leg hold traps; babies have their nest sites destroyed through construction, landscaping, or logging; for lack of natural habitat, their parents have chosen dangerous nest sites; or young birds are simply picked up when they shouldn't be.

CASCADES RAPTOR CENTER

Cascades Raptor Center provides high-quality medical treatment and rehabilitation to 300-700 sick, injured, and orphaned birds each year in the Louise Shimmel Wildlife Hospital. We receive birds from many sources — members of the public, veterinarians, state and local police, government agencies, and other wildlife rehabilitators. We have a responsibility, both to the birds and the people who bring them in, to provide the best care possible.

WHAT DOES A REHABILITATOR DO?

We are paramedics: stopping bleeding, treating for shock, providing emergency fluids, doing physical exams, immobilizing fractures, administering antibiotics.

We are laboratory technicians: drawing and analyzing blood for anemia, parasites, and signs of disease or starvation; analyzing fecal samples for parasites, bacteria, and blood; x-raying for fractures or other problems. Our staff veterinarian works with several generous off-site veterinarians who donate their services for surgery and consulting.

We are nurses: changing bandages and bedding, cleaning wounds, giving shots, administering medications.

We are dietitians: calculating the calories necessary for growth and healing, presenting the food in a way most conducive to self-feeding, making sure our patients are eating.

We are farmers: raising the live mice used for teaching birds to hunt.

We are custodians: hosing down carriers, washing dishes, disinfecting incubators, laundering bedding, cleaning constantly!

We are physical therapists: providing range of motion exercises to help loosen stiff joints and strengthen weakened muscles.

We are naturalists: utilizing our knowledge of a species's habitat, diet, and behavior in creating personalized treatment regimens for each bird.

And, finally, for each patient, we have to be the judges for a very difficult decision: Can this bird be released? Our first priority is always the welfare of the animal, and we must be confident that any bird we release is able to thrive in the wild

– to fly, catch food, find and defend a territory, attract a mate, reproduce, and migrate as appropriate to its species.

Our rehabilitation work is done under permits from both the Oregon Department of Fish & Wildlife and the US Fish & Wildlife Service. Cascades Raptor Center has a staff veterinarian who is also a licensed rehabilitator, with over twenty-five years of experience in wildlife medicine; we have also seven consulting veterinarians including board-certified avian, surgery, and ophthalmology specialists.

The Center is also very active in public education, with some forty permanent resident raptors on site. You can visit the birds during seasonal open hours, six days a week.

Cascades Raptor Center is a 501(c)3 non-profit organization and very much dependent on donations. If you would like to help these birds, please visit https://cascadesraptorcenter.org/